'I think it would have been incredible and it will be——'
His eyes burned with the certainty of it.

'Will be?' she echoed, her heart lurching with fear.

He smiled at the fear blazing in her vivid eyes.
'Inevitable,' he told her smoothly. 'You don't think two
beautiful people such as we can live together without
temptation taking a hand?'

'You really are the most arrogant man I've ever met,'
Fenella seethed breathlessly. 'You're also the stupidest.
You think I haven't seen through you? You wanted to
punish my father seven years ago but held back because
of my age and some peculiar stab of conscience; well,
there's nothing to stop you now, is there? Just one thing,
dear boy,' she husked sarcastically. 'The lady is no longer
willing! The rich spoilt teenager grew up to see through
bastards like you!'

DREAMS ARE FOR LIVING

BY

NATALIE FOX

MILLS & BOON LIMITED
ETON HOUSE   18-24 PARADISE ROAD
RICHMOND   SURREY   TW9 1SR

First published in Great Britain 1991
by Mills & Boon Limited

© Natalie Fox 1991

Australian copyright 1991
Philippine copyright 1991
This edition 1991

ISBN 0 263 77267 5

Set in Times Roman 11 on 12 pt.
01-9110-46857 C

Made and printed in Great Britain

CHAPTER ONE

FENELLA recognised him immediately. Seven years hadn't dimmed his image in her mind. Another seven wouldn't either, she thought grimly as her slender fingers whitened over the balustrade of the gallery.

The man with no name. A label had never figured in her fantasies. Even as she gazed down at him now she couldn't conjure one up for him. He could be a Trevelyan, a Cedric or a Xavier for all she knew. The man who had dramatically changed the course of her life could be plain old Sam, come to that.

So what was he doing here at Hunstand Manor, on the day of her father's wedding? She hadn't seen him at the church nor the reception held on the lawns of the family home by the river, but he was here now, a guest at the evening party her father, Joseph Trent the industrialist, was throwing before he set off for his honeymoon in the Seychelles.

'Seen someone that interests you?' her father said beside her. He put his arm around Fenella's bare shoulders, unconsciously twining a strand of her wild jet hair around his fingers. They both gazed over the gallery to the hall below where new guests were arriving. The double doors to the vast suite of reception-rooms were open and music, laughter and chatter combined into a medley of enjoyment. Joseph Trent's party were always like that: relaxed, informal and always, always a success.

'Not really,' Fenella exhaled deceptively. Never would she let on that the impressive man below who'd just arrived with his arm possessively locked around the minute waist of a living Barbie doll interested her in the slightest. Give Joseph Trent enough rope and he would have his only daughter lassoed into marriage before you could utter 'grandchildren'.

'Pity,' Joseph growled beside her. 'I never thought I'd see the day I'd be married before my own daughter.'

Fenella laughed and slid an arm around his ample waist. 'Hush, people might think I'm illegitimate.'

'You very nearly were, pet,' teased her father. 'Your mother had her doubts, right up until the very last minute. "Joe," she'd say, "people will say I'm marrying you for your money." She was on the factory floor, you see; never got over the fact that the boss had fallen in love with her.'

Leaning her head against him, Fenella murmured, 'I wish I could remember her—you always make her sound so lovely.' She turned her violet eyes to look at his still handsome face and asked, 'Did you think about her today?'

'Couldn't help it, could I?' he confessed gruffly. 'I make no apologies for it. I expect Adrianna was going through much the same. We both had happy marriages till fate intervened. When your mother died when you were a bairn I vowed there'd be no one else. Women to bed, yes, but never one to settle in my heart. As you know, Adrianna was my best friend's wife and when Geoff died she needed me.'

The perfect wife for her father, Fenella mused, turning her attention to another swarm of guests buzzing below. Like her own mother, Adrianna wouldn't give Joseph a hard time. She would be the dutiful wife, know her place in the home, and never, never pry into Joseph Trent's business empire. Fenella sighed inwardly. Her poor father, saddled with a daughter who definitely wasn't of that nature. She sometimes wished she were; it would make life simpler and there wouldn't be those awful arguments with him.

The man with no name, Barbie clinging to his arm, was raising a glass of champagne to his lips and looking decidedly bored. Fenella couldn't take her eyes off him and her father, ever perceptive, noticed.

'His name's Sam Ballantine,' he offered, a twinkle in his dark eyes.

Wincing at that, Fenella conceded that Sam was neither plain nor old.

'He has appalling taste in women,' she said tartly, which was more of a give-away than anything. She bit her lip for arousing her father's suspicions.

Joseph Trent chuckled. 'I think she's rather cute, but I must admit I'm rather surprised he brought anyone at all. The man has only been back in the country twenty-four hours; hardly time to establish a relationship with a woman.'

'Oh, I don't know, he looks a fast worker, all teeth and tan. Probably picked her up in the airport somewhere,' Fenella retorted.

'That was a bit below the belt.' With a laugh Joseph turned Fenella away from the balustrade. 'Come and have a few words with Adrianna before we leave.'

Glad to do anything but go downstairs and meet the new arrivals, Fenella walked with her father down the wide, thickly carpeted corridor to his bedroom, where Adrianna was changing into her going-away outfit.

She was also glad her father had not volunteered any more information about her fantasy man. She really didn't want to know why he was here, if he was a friend of her father or what he did for a living. She had never got over his rejection of her that sultry day seven years ago. It had been painful, intensely so, but in a way she was glad it had happened. Sam Ballantine didn't know it but he had been responsible for a dramatic change in the direction of her life. His bitter accusations, the contempt he held for her sort, had spurred her to prove to any man like him that she wasn't a rich spoilt bitch with an overload of hormones coursing her veins. She had a brain and a flair for business and was equal to any man in running a corporation.

Trouble was, convincing her father of that. Even after she'd set up her own investment management agency and made more money for herself than Joseph Trent paid his junior directors, he was still adamant. No women on the board. Fenella, in fury, had vowed to have that phrase engraved on his headstone!

'Adrianna, it looks perfect!' Fenella exclaimed at the sight of her lovely stepmother in the lilac silk dress with its matching jacket which she had helped her choose the week before.

Fenella hugged her. She loved Adrianna and was so happy for them both. Adrianna had always been like an aunty to her and Fenella couldn't have wished for a better match for her father. The only regret she had, and it was a purely selfish one, was that Adrianna shared her father's belief that a woman's place was in the home. Fenella would have welcomed an ally, someone to side with her and try to convince her father that she could be an asset on his board.

But the fact was that Adrianna was as eager for grandchildren as her beloved Joseph, and as Fenella was the sole offspring of them both— Adrianna and Geoff had never been blessed with children—it was down to her.

'You don't think it will be too hot when I arrive?' Adrianna asked anxiously, twirling uncertainly in front of the mirror.

'That's why we chose it,' Fenella reminded her with a laugh. 'You can slip off the jacket when you get there.' She wondered at Adrianna's anxiety. 'You sailed through the day, Adrianna; why so anxious now?' Suddenly her eyes sparkled and, giving her new stepmother an enormous wink, she teased, 'Or have you just realised what you've done? Actually married this man.' She tossed her head towards her father, who was watching his new bride with pride.

They all laughed at that and Adrianna let out a contented sigh and looked at her new husband with such deep love in her hazel eyes that Fenella felt a small pang of envy. If only she could find someone to love and trust so completely.

'To be honest, Fenella...' Adrianna smiled shyly, '...I'm not the greatest flier in the world and the Seychelles is so far away. At this moment in time a honeymoon in Brighton holds enormous appeal.'

'Now, darling, you know I only want the best for you, and Brighton just wouldn't suffice.' Joseph laughed. Taking her hands, he grinned down at her. 'You don't have to worry yourself—Joe will look after everything!'

That just about summed up their marriage for Fenella—Joe will look after everything! They loved each other, there was no doubt about that, but Adrianna needed her father to smooth her life for her, and Joseph Trent needed to be needed. He was quite confident that Adrianna's fear of flying couldn't possibly surface with him at her side. Fenella wondered how far Adrianna's request for a honeymoon in Brighton had got with him; probably no further than the M25!

Joseph Trent glanced at his watch. 'Time we were getting on. Now, Fenella, if you have any problems with the house call me at the hotel——'

'I'll do nothing of the sort,' Fenella retorted firmly. 'There are enough staff here to run a battle-ship. I foresee no problems, and don't forget,

Father, I have a business to run. If there is a hiccup here, it's for the housekeeper to sort out, not me...' Her voice trailed out as she caught a warning glint in Adrianna's eyes. Of course, she was right, this was no time to do battle with her father. 'Sorry, Dad.' She linked her arms around his neck and hugged him tight. 'Honeymoon time; forget you have a liberated daughter and enjoy.'

She hugged and kissed them both because once they got downstairs among the wedding guests there would be no chance for personal farewells. The three of them walked down the impressive curved stairway together, Joseph Trent between the two women. There was a cheer as they were noticed, and once among the guests at the foot of the stairs Fenella edged away from the happy couple. This was their time.

Instead, she went through to the huge, American-style kitchen where the caterers were putting the final touches to a sumptuous buffet.

'Everything all right, Joan?' Fenella asked the middle-aged housekeeper who was stacking plates ready to be taken through to the dining-room.

'Perfect. But I hope this is the last party in this house for a long time.' She sighed good-naturedly. 'I would have thought the wedding reception was enough without all this as well plus the guests staying on.'

Fenella frowned; her father hadn't mentioned anyone staying overnight, but then it was understandable. Some of them had come a long way to wish her father well and as always her father was the perfect host; overnight guests weren't unusual in Hunstand Manor.

'That's the price we have to pay for my father's being so popular,' she laughed. She slipped her arm around the housekeeper. 'And I bet you haven't had a decent cup of tea all day? I'm going to make you one.'

Gratefully sinking on to a stool, Joan rubbed the back of her hand across her forehead. 'You're right, I could murder a cuppa,' she breathed.

Fenella made her a good strong pot of tea and insisted that she drink the last drop. Then after checking that the caterers were on schedule she took a deep breath and joined the guests in the suite of reception-rooms that had been designed to open into one enormous room. In the last century it had served as a ballroom. This century it wasn't doing too badly either. Her father entertained a lot, held business meetings at the manor as well. That was when she had first seen him, Sam Ballantine. He had a name now, and Fenella rolled it silently round her lips.

'Fenny!'

Suddenly she was swung off her feet, the swirling taffeta of her short Emanuel party dress exposing the length of her silk-clad thighs and more! There were cat-calls, whistles of appreciation at the glimpse of her matching frilly briefs. But Fenella didn't care. She was among her dearest friends, the crazy wild crowd she had grown up with, sons and daughters of her father's wealthy business associates.

'Simon, darling!' she shrieked, grabbing at him for support and trying to smother him with kisses at the same time. It was then she caught the eye of Sam Ballantine over Simon's narrow shoulders. He was standing alone, in an unobstructed view of her across the room, and he recognised her, that was for sure. So if her friends had seen her underwear so had he! She turned as scarlet as her dress. Now he would know she hadn't changed a bit, and by the glowering black look he was giving her she would never get the chance to convince him otherwise. Did she want to? She snapped him out of her mind.

'Simon, you look wonderful, all brown and . . . and lovely.' She rumpled his sun-bleached hair. 'How's the Caribbean? I haven't seen you for over a year. Are you working or what?' The questions tumbled out of her excited red lips and her deep violet eyes were wide with pleasure. She thought she might be verging on hysteria, but through no fault of Simon's. She was delighted to see him, of course, but she knew instinctively that Sam Ballantine's eyes were still on her and some mysterious force was urging her to show off like mad!

'Work! What's that?' Simon hooted and swept her to the dance-floor where the pop group her father had hired had suddenly realised they were wearing their audience out with all their top ten hits and decided a soft smoochy number would be welcome.

'And talking of work . . .' Simon crushed her to him '. . . someone told me you've got yourself a little job. Don't tell me Daddy's millions are running out and poor Fenny has been forced out on to the streets?'

'An unfortunate choice of words, sonny,' came a low-timbred voice next to them. 'You make the lady sound like a woman of the night.' With a smooth movement Sam Ballantine eased Fenella from Simon's arms into his own.

Aghast, Simon went lobster under his tan. 'It . . . wasn't mean't . . . I mean, I didn't think anything of the sort . . .'

Fenella hardly heard his spluttering protestations; all she could hear was the rise and fall of Sam Ballantine's soft breath in her ear. Fire and fury combined to race her pulse. She forced him away from her with one push but he held on to her wrists.

'Simon meant nothing of the sort,' she blazed in defence of her friend, 'and if you don't mind we haven't seen each other for a year and——'

'And we haven't seen each other for seven,' he interrupted, his grey eyes lingering on the fullness of Fenella's mouth, familiarising himself with what he had turned away from all those years ago. 'I'm sure Simon will accept my apology and disappear while we catch up on old times.' He said it so smoothly and with such good humour that Simon grinned wickedly and, giving Sam a light slap on the back, left them to it.

With a sigh of pleasure that Fenella swore was highly exaggerated, Sam drew her softly into his arms again, softly yet forcibly. 'Inherited wealth and a thick skin often go together,' he mused in her ear. 'If I were in his shoes I would have punched me on the jaw for taking his woman from him.'

Fenella, stiff in his arms, hissed. 'And if I thought I could permeate your thick skin *I'd* punch you where it hurt, and I'm *not* his woman——'

'You were seven years ago; don't tell me after what I witnessed he didn't make an honest woman out of you.'

She tore herself from him then, her eyes wide and blazing with fury at the embarrassment the reminder caused her. She was speechless. What could you say to a man like this anyway? With a whirl of taffeta she spun on her high heels and left him in the middle of the dance-floor.

She ended up on the porch of the summer-house, where else? It had been her sanctuary since she was able to take her first steps. It had been there that her father had told her that Mummy had gone to heaven, there she had run to when she couldn't get her own way and then later, when puberty had forced its reluctant way on her, had taken her first cigarette, her first taste of alcohol, her first tentative step towards giving herself to Simon.

A deep shudder racked through her at the thought and, flopping sulkily down on to the swing sofa on the wooden porch, she rocked herself to and fro, gazing blindly out over the river that ran gently past the grounds of Hunstand Manor.

It was on such a day as this, hot and sultry, mid-August, when she had first seen the dark handsome stranger drive through the security gates at the end of the drive. She and Simon had just finished a game of tennis and had roared with laughter at the clapped-out old Mini that had shuddered to a halt in front of the house. Joan's husband, Dennis, who acted as chauffeur and butler, had greeted him with such a look of stern disapproval that Fenella and Simon had fallen against each other with mirth. The stranger had been dressed in jeans and his only concession to formality for her father's monthly business meeting was a white short-sleeved shirt, though crumpled in the heat of the day.

'Surely not one of your father's business associates?' Simon had guffawed. 'Maybe there's trouble at mill!'

He'd exploded at his own joke but for once Fenella had not responded. Sometimes she was sensitive to her roots. Her father was a northerner and proud of it. Their wealth wasn't inherited but came from the sheer hard work put in by her great-grandfather, who had founded Trent Steelworks, and her grandfather and father who had carried on to build the company into the vast corporation it was now.

Her father, although he had lived in the south for so long, still had traces of an accent. Fenella had never thought anything of it till it was pointed out to her by one of the girls at boarding-school. Puberty played hell with self-confidence and Fenella had been shattered at hearing her beloved father called a dowdy Geordie. Puberty also played hell with self-control; Fenella had lashed out, blacked Celia Braithwaite's eye, earning her lost privileges for a month and a stiff letter of disapproval from the school to her father. Her father had never mentioned it and neither had Fenella, but the incident had posed the thought inside her that if she had been born with a silver spoon up her nose like Celia she wouldn't have been so unladylike as to have thrown a punch her way. It was just one small thought that nurtured a change in Fenella; the rest was to come directly from that tall dark stranger who'd defied the establishment by turning up to a business meeting in jeans.

'Come on, I'll race you to the river. I need to cool off.' Simon had shouted and headed towards the summer-house where he'd left his gear.

'Wait for me, Simon. I have to go to the house for my bikini,' she'd wailed.

'See you by the jetty, then, and hurry up, Sean and Cathy are punting up from Marlow to join us for the picnic lunch Joan promised.'

She had watched him as he'd loped off down the gravel path towards the summer-house. Tall, narrow and very handsome. They had practically grown up together. He was the only son of their neighbours, the Taylor-Parkeses, landowners since medieval days. Simon was on his own a lot and tended to spend much of his school holidays at Hunstand Manor with Fenella. They had a lot in common. Both loved tennis and swimming and had the same taste in gory videos.

Turning, Fenella had run off towards the house. Maybe she would get a closer look at that gorgeous man, find out what he was doing here.

She'd been disappointed when she had skidded into the front hall and found that her father and his associates were already closeted in his study. She'd pressed her ear to the door and heard the familiar rumble of male voices, the clink of coffee-cups.

Not bothering to change from her brief white tennis shorts and T-shirt, she'd grabbed her bikini and flung herself downstairs again in the hope that someone might come out of the study, giving her a glimpse into the inner sanctum and sight of *him*. Again she had been disappointed and desolately turned down the corridor to the kitchen to make sure Dennis was bringing their picnic hamper down to the summer-house.

He was coming out of the double swing doors to the kitchen with a glass of iced water, the tall dark stranger who was even more devastatingly handsome close-up. Shyness wasn't one of Fenella's weaknesses and she opened her mouth to give him a cheery greeting, but the words stuck in her throat as he strode past her as if she were the ghost that was rumoured to haunt the old manor. If she had been that ghost she might have had more impact on the man. He was glowering, that was the only description that fitted his face, glowering darkly, clutching the water and striding back to the study.

To her astonishment Fenella found herself trembling, half with rage at being ignored and half with excitement. He was male, all male, with springy black hair that straddled his collar, a mouth that, though severe, looked as if it held sensual promise. Eyes of steel-grey, skin taut and lightly tanned as if he spent time out of doors, a bone-structure of near perfection, a jawline of power. His shoulders were wide, his arms heavily muscled, as were the legs that strode away from her, stretching worn denim to its limits. She saw all this and more in perhaps three seconds of her life and it affected her profoundly.

Fenella slumped back against the wall and closed her eyes for a second to try and calm her racing heartbeat. So that was what all the girls at school were always raging on about: sex appeal. He was the stuff of the romantic novels which she and her friends devoured by the crateful. *The* hero, the male chauvinist, the lover.

She forgot to remind Dennis of the picnic hamper and this time she didn't run anywhere but strolled lazily down to the summer-house. Her head swam with sensations, the nature of which she wasn't mature enough to recognise, but she knew she felt different, oddly different.

Stripping off her tennis gear in the summer-house, she stood naked in front of a long mirror. She hoped she'd stopped growing upwards but not outwards. Her breasts were still small, much smaller than her friends'. Was it all over by sixteen? Would she develop any more? She looked like a boy:

narrow-hipped, long-limbed, almost rangy. Her hair was her only strikingly feminine feature. Black as jet, it gleamed and fell in silky waves around her oval face, brushing her tanned shoulders. She wondered about her face, leaned towards the mirror to examine it. Was she pretty? Last week Simon had surprised her with a blushing statement saying she was beautiful. She had laughed at that. Her eyes were unusual though—deep violet, thickly fringed with dark lashes. She hated her mouth; her lips were too full and she practised putting lipstick on inside her lip-line to make them look smaller. She'd read that in a magazine. It didn't seem to work.

'Fenny! Hurry up, the others are coming.'

She heard Simon's step on the wooden boards of the veranda outside and leapt into her bikini bottoms with fright. She didn't quite make the top though and there was a horrible awkward silence before Simon spluttered an apology and Fenella clipped the back clamp with trembling fingers.

'S... sorry. I... I thought you were ready.' His eyes raked her slender body, and, though he had seen her near naked before, they both sensed that this time it was different.

Flushed, Simon rushed outside, yelling unnaturally to the others as they tied their punt up at the small jetty.

Later they swam together, four friends who had known each other through childhood. Fenella remembered floating on her back in the warm river water and gazing up into blue, blue skies. This year was different, this summer hotter. She swam back to the jetty, sat on the edge and swished her legs in the brownish water, gazed in awe at a butterfly that landed in the reeds next to her. Wild-life had never interested her before but now, suddenly, she was fascinated.

He had done that to her, she mused; the dark stranger had opened her eyes to the wonders of the world. But why, and why couldn't it have been Simon who made her feel this way?

They ate their picnic lunch and drank wine her father had allowed them and they laughed and joked around in the hazy heat of the afternoon. Sean and Cathy wandered off for a walk along the river-bank and she and Simon stretched lazily in the heat of the sun and then it happened, that strange unaccountable sequence of events that had changed her life.

Now Fenella got up from the swing seat and stood against the veranda post, shivering in spite of the balmy night. Laughter and music reached her ears, muted by distance but a reminder that there was still a world out there. She tried to think of her father and Adrianna, at the airport by now, taking champagne in the first-class lounge. The airport, where only a day ago Sam Ballantine had arrived. Oh, why had he come, to taunt her with reminders of that excruciating incident? And he would taunt her; hadn't he mentioned it already?

She didn't want to think about it but it was impossible, had been impossible for the last seven years. Each time she unwillingly brought it back to mind she hoped her memory would dredge up something she had forgotten, some face-saving incident that would ease her guilt, but it never had. In Sam Ballantine's eyes she had appeared a promiscuous little tramp and all the memory-dredging wouldn't alter that.

'I'm surprised this place is still standing,' a soft voice murmured only feet from her. 'It was a tumbledown shack last time I was here.'

With a start Fenella strained her eyes in the darkness. The temptation to run was strong but her anger at his nerve for coming to this place outweighed her cowardice.

'It's been rebuilt. What do you want?' she husked into the night air.

'You left me looking an idiot in the middle of the dance-floor. I came to claim the rest of the dance.' He swung up the three steps towards her and clasped her once again in his arms. 'If you concentrate, you can just about hear the music from here.'

She pushed him away, one hand on the front of his dinner-jacket to hold him off, the other gripping the wooden post for support. 'I don't want to dance with you,' she breathed vehemently. 'Go back to your Barbie girlfriend, or is she your wife?'

'Someone else's, actually,' he grated, and Fenella suppressed the gasp of shock that rose in her throat. 'I've sent her back home in a taxi so that you can have my undivided attention for the rest of the night.'

'What makes you think for a second that I want it?' she retorted, and knew with a sickening plunge of her heart that she had said the wrong thing. She could hardly see him in the darkness but she could feel him, feel the arrogant thrust of his shoulders, feel the mockery oozing from his very being.

'My, my. We have changed, haven't we? There was a time you begged for it,' he reminded her softly.

She held back, her temper, her tears. 'I was a child then, so you eloquently told me. What were the exact words? "A rich spoilt brat with an excess of hormones..."'

'"Who thinks she can seduce grown men but in fact has the sex appeal of an anorexic boa constrictor",' he finished for her. 'Well, darling, I must admit you've filled out since then and you're not about to spit poison, or are you?'

'I wish that I had that capability,' she hissed venomously, and tried to push past him.

He caught her, swung her back against the post, stood so close that she was assailed by his warmth and heady masculine scent. 'You're a woman now, Fenella, a stunning one. I wonder, does that offer of seven years ago still stand?'

A sliver of cold fear iced down her spine. Just one touch and she couldn't be sure, that was how deeply he had affected her all those years ago. If he lowered his lips to hers, would she melt as she had done in her fantasies?

'Does your silence imply that it does?' he murmured. His hand came up and stroked her hair. It crackled with the *frisson* of electricity that surged between them. She jerked her head away, terrified he might go further and touch her skin.

Over the years she had disciplined herself to reject every advance that had come her way, and there had been many, but this man, back in her life, was proving that she had suppressed a natural need. She ached to be loved, but had locked away that need because one hot and sultry day, a lifetime ago, this man had made her feel cheap and dirty.

She wished she could see his face, was glad he couldn't see hers. She stiffened herself and lifted her chin defiantly.

'I wish I had your talent for words, Sam Ballantine, but sadly I can't think of anything more original to say than *drop dead*!'

She pushed past him and he stepped aside, plunging his hands deep into his trouser pockets. She knew he was watching her hurry away, back to the house and her father's wedding party. She heard his soft laughter, low-timbred and heavy in the warm night air. It channelled fear deep inside her, had sounded like a gauntlet being thrown softly down at her feet.

As she neared the house and the welcoming sound of other people's laughter she shook off that fear. She was over-reacting. After tonight she would never see Sam Ballantine again, not unless her father married again, and that wasn't likely. One thought clouded her resolve to enjoy the rest of the night. Why on earth had her father invited him anyway?

CHAPTER TWO

FENELLA woke with a headache to end all headaches. Serves you right, she grimaced as she surfaced from a bundle of tangled sheeting. It was midday. With alarm she went to sprint from the bed but in agony and relief she slumped back against the pillows. It was Sunday. Her only day of rest. She groped feebly for the phone.

'Oh, Joan,' she groaned into the mouthpiece, 'send Karen up with some black coffee, there's a darling.'

There was unsympathetic laughter from Joan who had been so long with the family that she was a part of it. 'You know champagne doesn't agree with you; why did you do it?'

'Was that what I was drinking? This morning I could swear it was meths. Tell me, Joan, did I have a good time?'

Joan laughed again. 'You were the belle of the ball. By the way, it's Sunday, remember, and your father gave all the staff the rest of the weekend off...' there was a small pause which Fenella in her state of agony hardly registered '...but Mr Ballantine here has offered to bring your coffee up.'

'I don't care if Quasimodo humps it up,' Fenella moaned. 'Just tell him to make it quick.' She rattled the receiver back into its cradle and turned her throbbing head back into the pillow. Belle of the ball, was she...? Oh, my God!

She was up in an instant, rocking with shock and grasping the bedpost for support. Had she heard right? Mr Ballantine?

She lunged at the telephone, Joan must have made a mistake. There was a rap at the door and in fright Fenella dropped the phone with a crash. She only had time to slip her satin wrap-over round her shoulders to cover her nakedness before he was in the room.

Shocked into numbness, Fenella stood as still as a statue, the robe clutched tightly to her. Not in her wildest fantasies could she have dreamed this up. Here he was, in her bedroom, walking towards her with a loaded tray and a smile on his face. To her astonishment he was still wearing the black trousers and finely pleated white evening shirt he'd worn the night before. He'd been here all night! Of all the nerve!

'Just what do you think you're playing at?' she croaked, tightening her grip on the oyster satin as he put the tray on the bedside table.

'Emulating a faithful family retainer, I would say, wouldn't you?' he replied smoothly. 'But don't think I'm going to make a habit of this. It's your turn tomorrow.'

'To...tomorrow?'

'Bank holiday, and my turn for a lie-in.' Calmly and coolly he poured her coffee then handed her a glass of fresh orange juice. 'Drink this first. Vitamin C is the best cure for a hangover.'

'I can think of a better one,' she retorted. 'You! My headache has miraculously cleared. Now will you kindly tell me what you are still doing here? Or is that a silly question? Were you so drunk you forgot where you live?' she gibed sarcastically.

He laughed. 'You were the one that was running wild last night. No, I wasn't drunk. I felt it my duty to stay sober and keep an eye on you. Don't forget. I know what happens to little girls who can't hold their liquor.'

She flushed deeply at that reminder. Would she ever be rid of that terrible day? She turned away and carried the juice over to the window to finish it. She turned as he slumped down on to her bed and poured himself a cup of coffee. Two cups he had brought up to her bedroom. How dared he?

'I wasn't drunk then and I wasn't drunk last night. It was my father's wedding night and I had reason to celebrate. I have a low tolerance level for champagne,' she explained, gazing out of the french windows at the moody river and wondering if she would wake up in a minute and find this was all a nightmare.

'And what was your excuse seven years ago? If I remember it was white wine then, an Alsace Riesling if my memory serves me—— '

'Shut up!' she cried with such force that he did. There was a long, long silence then which Fenella filled with trying to purge every second of that August day from her tortured mind. He had got it all so terribly wrong, misconstrued the whole scene. And she hadn't been drunk, but she had to admit the wine had dazed her a little, that and the heat and the strange new feelings inside her...

'Don't, that tickles,' she had murmured lazily to Simon as he had stroked a blade of dry grass over her stomach. Dreamily she had opened her eyes and saw Simon gazing down at her with such a strange look in his soft blue eyes that she had giggled. She rolled over on her stomach, leaned her chin on the back of her hands and stared at the long grass growing up the side of the summer-house and thought of the handsome stranger up at the house.

Simon's hand smoothed over her back and she didn't giggle any more. Gently he turned her towards him and leaned over to kiss her. It was her first serious kiss and she thought it the most beautiful feeling in the world. She lost herself in its sweetness and only surfaced when she felt Simon tremble against her. She felt floaty and the sun felt good on her face and bare legs. She let Simon touch her then, a light, hesitant caress over her bikini top and then more as his inexperienced fingers shook against the bare flesh he had exposed. And then everything around her fast-forwarded as if someone had triggered a remote control. Simon made an odd guttural sound deep in his throat as a shadow dropped over them. He fled and Fenella was hauled to her feet.

'Cover yourself up, for God's sake!' the tall, dark stranger ordered. 'How old are you, fifteen? You've got to be out of your mind!'

She argued and screamed at him, rushed into the summer-house and threw her tennis T-shirt over her nakedness. He was outside when she burst out of the summer-house. Bravado spurred by embarrassment oiled her words till they slid from her lips like ball-bearings.

'Does my father know you're spying on me...? I've heard of your sort; is that how you get you kicks...?'

Oh, there was more, much more, till at last he burst out laughing at the, 'I'll have you horse-whipped by my father!' bit. Then came his 'rich spoilt brat' soliloquy followed by the one thing she was to wish she had never done. She blatantly stepped up to him and slid her arms up around his neck.

'Hypocrite,' she murmured languidly, not aware of the sexy huskiness of her voice. 'Don't tell me you don't find me attractive. Why don't you kiss me and put us both out of our misery?'

She thought dazedly afterwards that she must have read that or heard it in a film somewhere but, whatever, she had said it and the stranger had looked at her as if she had crawled out of a rotting log.

Fenella gripped the orange juice glass in her two hands with such force that she nearly splintered it. She felt warm fingers on hers, easing it from her grasp. Back to the present, she stared blankly at Sam Ballantine.

'Drink your coffee before it gets cold,' he told her gently. He put it down on her dressing-table by the window and quietly walked out of the room.

He knew, Fenella thought fretfully as she gulped the bittersweet coffee, knew what I was thinking and how guilty and embarrassed I still feel. Yet it hadn't stopped him tormenting her. She shuddered at the thought of what he didn't know and never would, another unbearable realisation she'd had to battle with over the years. Poor Simon, how she had used him that day. It hadn't been him kissing her and caressing her breast, it had been the dark stranger she now knew to be Sam Ballantine. In her imagination, like some Greek mythological god, he had taken on Simon's form. And the worst realisation of all was that the fantasy had been so real that it wouldn't have stopped when the real Sam Ballantine had stood over them. She would have let Simon make love to her that afternoon on the river-bank, as a substitute for the stranger, and that thought tortured her. There had to be something wrong with her; she wasn't normal, she wasn't like other girls.

Letting out a small sob of anguish, Fenella rushed to the bathroom and twisted the bathtaps on full. She'd tried to forget him that hot summer, but it had been hopeless. He'd spoiled her relationship with Simon; he hadn't come near her till the Christmas holidays and then they had never spoken of the incident. And the stranger had shattered her adolescent confidence in herself. She'd felt cheap and unattractive and lost even more weight till she was in fact verging on anorexia. It was only the threat from her father to bring in a psychologist that had snapped her out of her depression. No, she wasn't mad, but she had been stupid to let that stranger affect her life so deeply, and there was only one way to get out of that. Work.

Fenella lay in the hot bath and closed her eyes. It had been her salve; university, an economics degree, a flair for business that had shaken her father. And at twenty-three, her own investment company made up of like-thinking women whom she had met at university. Fenella denied hotly that she was a feminist—her all-girl staff came about simply because all the male applicants for the job had turned it down because the boss was a woman! But investors, eager to make money, held no such anti-feminist convictions. The business, to her father's amused chagrin, had thrived. But was Fenella satisfied? She wished she was, but the truth was she wanted to stretch herself further, wanted into her father's company.

She dried herself and dressed quickly in 501s and a floppy black T-shirt. Bending over and raking her fingers through her mass of layered jet hair to give it more body, she paused in thought. What had he meant by 'it's your turn tomorrow'? Anyone would think he was planning on staying the whole Bank Holiday weekend. She straightened up, shook her hair around her shoulders. No way, José!

He was coming out of her father's study with his dinner-jacket looped over one shoulder and his bowtie hanging loose around his open collar when she reached the bottom of the stairs.

'And what are you doing in my father's study?' she tackled haughtily. 'Don't tell me you slept in there?'

'I slept in the room next to yours, as it happened.' He grinned, his eyes crinkling at the corners in such a way that Fenella's hurt lurched. 'But I had some overseas phone calls to make after the party broke up, used the study and left my jacket behind.'

'I hope you intend to pay for those calls. My father isn't a mean man but I hardly think he would approve of a stranger running up colossal bills while he's away.' She gave him one of her sternest looks which he met with a puzzled frown. His mouth opened as if to say something but with a shrug he changed his mind, drew his lips into that severe thin line she remembered so well.

'I rather think that's between me and your father,' he told her brittly. 'Now, I hate to have to ask, but could you possibly give me a lift to my home? I've tried for a taxi but nothing is available for another half-hour and I am rather pushed for time.'

Fenella smiled, rather smugly. 'Nothing would give me greater pleasure.' At last he was going. She must have misunderstood about her turn for breakfast the next day. 'But I hope it's not too far, I'm rather pushed for time myself.' She glanced at her watch, inwardly cursed herself for over-sleeping. She had work to do. Normally she kept Sundays free for relaxation but during the week a virtually unknown company had been arousing great interest on the Stock Exchange and before she invested anyone's money she wanted to check into them.

'So, you haven't got a car? Did the Mini finally collapse with exhaustion?' she asked as they crunched across the gravel drive to the garages at the rear of the manor. There was a way through the house, down the corridor and past the kitchen, but Fenella wanted him out as quick as possible and the front door was just there.

'The Mini?' He frowned and then remembered and glanced at her curiously. 'You didn't miss much that day, did you?'

She curbed a flush of anger with herself for that. 'Simon and I thought you hysterical, arriving in that heap and in jeans too,' she cut spitefully.

'Yes, I suppose I must have looked odd,' was all he said, which made Fenella feel an even bigger fool.

She skidded her white BMW Cabriolet, the top already down, out of the garage and waited while he got in then shot down the drive at such a speed that the wind whipped his loose bowtie into the back seat. He retrieved it hastily and stuffed it into his pocket.

'Hired?' she asked sweetly, unable to resist digging at him at every opportunity.

'Time hasn't taught you much, has it, Fenella? You're still that spoilt bitch you were when you were fifteen.' His eyes were straight ahead on the security gates looming up.

'Sixteen, actually,' she iced back, pushing her shame at probably embarrassing him to the back of her mind. So what if he couldn't afford his own evening suit; lots of people hired... Oh, damn him!

Fenella opened the gates by remote control. 'Left or right?'

'I'm not sure. I arrived last night in a taxi and didn't take much notice...'

'Well, surely you know where you live?' She revved the engine impatiently.

He grinned and his grey eyes crinkled. 'I bought the house over the phone. I only arrived back in the country on Friday night, far too exhausted to take notice of where I was going.' He stretched lazily in the passenger-seat, raised his face to the hot sun. 'It's a lovely day. We'll just have to drive around in the hope I might recognise it.'

'Look, this isn't Trent tours, you know!' she exploded. 'I thought you were in a hurry? You must have some idea where it is?'

He rubbed his forehead in an exaggerated expression of trying to remember. Fenella drummed her nails on the steering-wheel.

'Ah, yes. The village of Brampton, or is it Bramley, or Brim——?'

'Bramley!' she interrupted with relief, shot the gear into first and turned left. It was only ten minutes' drive away, only ten more minutes of suffering him.

'Nice car,' he mused after a few miles. 'Present from Daddy?'

A protestation that she had bought the car out of her own hard-earned salary died on her lips. What did it matter? He obviously didn't think she was capable of supporting herself, so why bother trying to impress him otherwise? She ignored the question, slammed the gear into third and took a corner a racing driver would have been proud of. To her delight Sam Ballantine paled.

'This looks familiar,' he said after a few more miles. 'Slow down. I think it's that lane over there.'

Fenella swung over the road and into a narrow track passing a signpost to Lytton Grange. Fenella frowned. Surely he hadn't bought the Grange? It had been on the market for aeons, the asking price ludicrously high, too high for the likes of Sam Ballantine. She vaguely wondered what he did for a living, but didn't bother to ask because shortly she would be rid of him and wasn't likely to see him again.

'Whoa! Too far. You'll have to back up.'

She muttered a silent curse. The reverse gear was so stiff that she always had a struggle. She fluffed it and at the next attempt his hand closed over hers and firmly guided the gear-stick for her. His hand was hot on hers and she tried to ease it from under his but he held on as she backed up a few yards. The heat of the contact travelled her arm and surged through her body. Slamming the gear into first, she let out the clutch too quickly and stalled the engine.

He took his hand away with a smile of satisfaction, knowing the contact had thrown her. Fenella wanted to slap the smile from his face.

The cottage she pulled up in front of with a jolt was hideous. Even the bright sunshine did nothing to gladden the plain red brick of its structure. Well, she hadn't expected Lytton Grange, but she hadn't expected this hovel either.

'Bought it over the phone, did you?' she quipped. 'I'm not surprised. One sight of this and they couldn't have given it away.'

He laughed at that, not in the least put off by her show of distaste.

'It'll be all right when it's been touched up a bit.' He opened the door and slid out. 'Do you want to come in and wait or sit here in the car?'

Violet eyes widened in surprise. 'Wait? For what?'

He looked sheepish, raked a hand through his dark hair. 'I need to change out of these clothes and pack a few things. I haven't organised a car yet. I'm afraid I'll have to ask for another lift.'

With a sigh of exasperation Fenella switched of the engine. 'This is ridiculous!' She folded her arms across her chest. 'Well, hurry up. I haven't got all day!'

She watched him stroll over what had once been a front garden, now strewn with old bedsprings with nettles growing through them. He was in no hurry and Fenella fumed as he picked his way through the debris to the front door, a strange sight in full evening dress.

Ten minutes later, she was still waiting, hot and sticky and on the verge of leaving him there.

'This is taking longer than I expected,' he called from a downstairs window. 'The kettle's on, would you like to make some coffee?'

Thirst drove her to accept his invitation reluctantly and, besides, she admitted to herself equally reluctantly, she was mildly curious.

As she got out of the car a lorry, loaded with building materials, chuggered up the lane towards the Grange. So, someone had bought the rambling old house, was obviously having it gutted. Some people had more money than sense, she mused, skirting the bedsprings. The Grange had the reputation of being a Victorian folly that only a rich crank would consider buying.

And Sam Ballantine must have been out of his mind to have bought this place, Fenella thought, as she stopped in the dim hallway. The smell of damp and rotting woodwork was almost overpowering. The thought of brewing coffee here sent a shudder through her.

'Where's the kitchen?' she called out, and started as he came out of one of the downstairs rooms. She looked past him to see that the room wasn't as bad as she had expected it might be. Though it was piled high with packing cases, the sun filtered in, brightening it considerably.

'Down the end. The agent had it cleaned up a bit and there's instant coffee and a carton of milk in a box on the table.'

He'd already changed into jeans, more than likely the same jeans he'd worn seven years ago by the state of them, and a white T-shirt that still held creases where it had been folded. Some of the packing cases were open with an array of clothing hanging from them and a suitcase lay on the floor near by. Next to the suitcase lay a cardboard box with the name of a well-known dress hire company on the side. Sam Ballantine's evening suit was neatly packed into it. Remorse, for her insensitive remarks, knifed through her.

She walked past him to the kitchen, surprised that her heart pulled so tightly at the sight of such disarray. If he'd arrived on Friday he must have spent the night here and she wouldn't have wished that on her worst enemy. No wonder he'd stayed last night at the manor; this place was awful.

The kitchen wasn't quite awful. Someone in the past had made an attempt at modernisation and it was clean. The sun shone through a cracked glass window and Fenella peered out into the back garden which was as wild and unkempt as the front. He'd have his work cut out making this place habitable, she thought, as she found the coffee and two mugs in the box on an old pine table.

Two mugs, she mused, as she waited for the kettle to boil on an old gas stove by the door. Had he planned on bringing his Barbie here? She frowned at that thought.

'I think we'll drink it outside,' he said as he joined her in the kitchen. 'It's so stuffy in here.' He wrenched open the back door, which shuddered on its hinges.

'How many sugars?' she asked, peering into the box.

'None,' he called from outside.

'Just as well,' Fenella muttered, 'there isn't any.'

She took the coffees outside, joined him on a rickety bench seat against the back wall of the house. He sat back with his legs stretched out in front of him, his face upturned to the warm sun, eyes closed. He hadn't shaved that morning and blue growth caught the light. He looked jet-lagged in spite of the deep tan.

'I understand you've been living abroad,' she said quietly. 'By the look of the tan, somewhere exotic.'

'The Middle East for the last two years. The five years before that, the States.' He murmured his reply without opening his eyes.

Seven years altogether. A creepy sensation nettled down Fenella's back. All the time she had imagined he might walk back into her life, he hadn't even been in the country!

'So now you know where I've been since we last met; what about you? From what I overheard from lover-boy, you've got yourself a little job. Daddy set you up in an exclusive boutique somewhere, did he?'

Anger flared and died. His attitude was despicable yet understandable. Daughters of wealthy fathers usually ended up doing something equally puerile while sitting around waiting to be married off to a suitably rich suitor. If her father had had his way that would indeed have been her fate, as it had been of most of her girlfriends at the exclusive boarding-school she had attended. Little did Sam Ballantine know that his callous attitude years ago had forced her into proving she wasn't one of those idle socialites. But she wasn't going to admit to that, not to him or anyone.

'I've kept myself occupied, yes,' she told him non-commitally.

He opened his eyes then. 'And you never married?'

'Never met anyone who could keep me in the style I've been accustomed to,' she frosted back, unable to resist giving him what he obviously wanted to hear. It wasn't worth being truthful with a man like him. Chauvinists hated challenge from a liberated woman. Much as she loved her father, he was the epitome of male chauvinism; it was akin to banging her head against a brick wall trying to convince him that she had a brain on a par with those of his other directors.

They finished their coffee in silence and then with a frown Sam Ballantine glanced at his watch. 'We really ought to get going.'

'Where do you want me to drop you? The Abingdon?' It was a hotel close by. Suddenly Fenella froze. A huge black cat with a small army of kittens gambolling around it stepped out of the undergrowth that nearly reached to the back door. She leapt to her feet, letting go of the mug and spilling the dregs of the coffee down the front of her jeans.

With a surprised laugh, Sam bent down and scooped up one of the kittens and thrust it into Fenella's chest. 'It's only a domestic cat, not a black panther, you know.'

Taken by surprise, Fenella clutched at the kitten to stop it falling to the ground, held it to her chest for one brief second but it was long enough. With a strangled sob she cast it from her.

With a gasp of fury, Sam caught the kitten before it hit the ground, gently set it down on the grass and turned to her, eyes metallic with outrage.

'Are you crazy? You nearly killed the poor little thing. Terrified of it dirtying your bloody designer T-shirt?' he yelled at her.

Grasping at her throat, her eyes streaming, Fenella tried to talk. Her chest heaved with the effort and suddenly the ground at her feet started to crawl its way up to her.

'Oh, my God,' Sam raked hoarsely, catching her before she fell.

Fenella grabbed at him and clung on as he helped her inside the house. For an instant she blacked out with the effort of gasping for breath. When she came round she was in the room with the packing cases, stretched out on a battered sofa with Sam supporting her head and shoulders in his arms. She lay there, feeling oddly safe and secure, till gradually the colour flushed back into her ashen face.

'Don't try and speak. I'm sorry, darling, I had no idea.' Gently he smoothed the wild tumble of hair from her face. 'Have you anything with you: some tablets, an inhaler?'

Miserably, she shook her head, her eyes streaming with tears brought on by the attack. Gently he laid her back against the bulging sofa. 'I'll get you some water.'

In the seconds it took him to get to the kitchen, Fenella fought the attack with every ounce of strength she possessed. Why did that have to happen in front of him? He was the last person she wanted to show weakness and vulnerability to.

He came back with the water, held it to her mouth as she sipped the cool liquid. Her hands shook as she tried to grasp the mug he held to her lips.

'Good grief! Look at your hands.'

Already the rash was appearing where the kitten's fur had made contact. Fenella tried to hide them in the folds of her T-shirt but he grasped them and held them to his lips in such a moment of tenderness that Fenella wanted to cry.

'It will go in a minute,' she croaked, her throat dry with the effort of speaking. 'The severest case of allergy the specialist has ever seen,' she explained, trying to raise a smile.

He looked at her with such fierce tenderness that Fenella thought another attack was imminent.

'It doesn't last long,' she explained, oddly wanting to reassure him. 'And I haven't had an attack for years. I just steer clear of cats,' she finished weakly.

'You'd better get out of that T-shirt,' he said gently. 'It's covered in the kitten's fur.' He stood up and started raking feverishly through a tea-chest and came out with a dishevelled shirt.

Gently he eased her to a sitting-up position, slid her floppy black T-shirt over her head. Instinctively she clutched at her naked breasts, fear clouding the violet of her eyes.

'Don't be afraid, Fenella,' he husked, his eyes smoky with dismay at the look in her eyes. 'Don't ever be afraid of me.'

Slowly he wrapped his shirt around her shoulders, eased her trembling hands into the armholes. She strove to relax to make his job easier, closed her eyes so as not to meet his. His touch fired every pulsing nerve in her body, every nerve-ending she had fought so long to keep frozen within her.

'Sam,' she moaned as his fingers brushed her skin in his attempt to do up the buttons. He hesitated for an instant, withdrew his fingers from their task. Then she felt his warm breath on her breast, his lips caress her heated flesh. She moaned his name one more time before his mouth closed over her nipple, ran his tongue over its hardened silkiness.

Her back arched in ecstasy and seven years of her life rolled away from her. This was real, her frustrated fantasy coming to fulfilment. Her hands came up and her fingers raked through his thick hair. She opened her eyes as he raised his head and their eyes met in agonised silence. When he lowered his mouth to hers it was exactly as she had always imagined it would be. Soft, sensual and as warm as the sun on her face that day long ago.

Weakened by her allergy attack, she was forced to gasp for breath before either of them were satisfied. Her mouth moved exhaustedly from his mouth to the stubble on his cheek. Whether or not he took this as rejection she never knew, for suddenly he moved jerkily away from her.

'I'll finish my packing,' he said hoarsely, as if *he* were suffering from some stricture of the throat.

He moved restlessly around the room, grabbing things from different boxes and ramming them haphazardly into his suitcase. Fenella closed her eyes again, to exhausted to analyse or delve too deeply into what had just happened. All she knew was that shame and guilt for letting her needs run away with her were creeping over her flesh again. Eventually she blinked open her eyes when he snapped shut the lock on the cases. She got to her feet, still a little dizzy.

He came and stood before her, tall and dark and so unreadable that she bit her lip in anguish. She had given so much away, so much of herself that she had wanted to keep buried within her.

'I'll drive,' he told her gently, holding his hand out for the car keys.

'The keys are in the car,' she told him weakly. She would have to get a taxi back from the hotel. She'd never be able to drive in this condition and it wasn't altogether to do with her allergy attack. Sam Ballantine had shaken all the strength from her.

They reached the end of the track and turned into the lane, Fenella sitting weakly in the passenger-seat. A few miles later she narrowed her anguished violet eyes and turned to him.

'You really don't know your way about these parts, do you? This isn't the way to the Abingdon Hotel.'

He took his eyes from the road to look at her with that detached puzzlement he had used back at the manor when she had challenged him over the overseas phone calls he had made.

'You don't know, do you?' he said gravely, his eyes shifting back to the road.

Unease moved restlessly down her spine. She stiffened, glanced nervously at the side of his face. His jaw muscles were tight, almost in anger.

'I don't understand. What do you mean, I don't know?' she asked in a whisper barely audible over the breeze that had gathered and was rushing past them.

Sam Ballantine's hands gripped the steering-wheel forcibly, a small gesture that unnerved Fenella.

'I suppose he forgot to tell you, what with the excitement of the wedding——'

'You mean my father; what did he forget to tell me?' Fenella cried in exasperation.

'Your father invited me to live at the manor for as long as it takes for my new home to be refurbished.'

'He did what?' Fenella gasped in amazement. Never for a moment had she suspected that. But surely there must be a mistake. For all she knew her father hadn't clapped eyes on Sam Ballantine since that hot August day seven years ago. And yet . . . he'd been an invited guest at the wedding party.

Fenella rubbed her forehead in sheer frustration. 'Why should he do that?'

Sam overtook a lorry down the narrow lane, and didn't speak till they were on clear road again.

'I think that's for your father to explain, not me.'

'That's it, is it?' Fenella gasped. 'You're not going to explain any further?'

Obviously not. There wasn't another word from Sam Ballantine till he asked how to operate the security gates of Hunstand Manor.

'Thanks,' he muttered after she had mumbled the code to be punched into the remote control. 'I shall be in and out of here a lot over the next few months.'

Fenella forgot his sensuous caresses and the kiss that had bridged all those lonely years this hot afternoon. A few months with Sam Ballantine in the house was going to be unbearably frustrating, for she knew that he wasn't going to be there because he wanted to be near her. No, this had all been planned well beforehand. Something was going on between this man and her father and she wanted to know exactly what it was. And she would find out, Sam Ballantine need have no fear of that. She would phone her father as soon as she got inside the house. Joseph Trent had some explaining to do.

CHAPTER THREE

FURIOUSLY Fenella slammed down the receiver. 'How can he do this to me?'

'Do what?' Sam asked behind her.

Fenella swung round to face him, her eyes bright with anger and sheer amazement.

'He's not at the hotel in Mahé. He arrived and then promptly took a boat over to one of the other islands, won't be back till Thursday.'

'Well, it is his honeymoon, you know.'

'Of course I damned well know!' Fenella snapped at him. She raked her hair back from her face and slumped into her father's study chair. She looked up at Sam Ballantine standing in front of the mahogany desk. 'You'd better start explaining because for sure I'm not waiting till Thursday to find out what's going on,' she seethed through tight lips.

He shook his dark head, splayed his hands on her father's desk and leaned towards her. 'Explain what? Isn't it enough for you that your father was kind enough to offer me some decent accommodation——'

'No, it's not!' Fenella shot to her feet. 'This is my home you expect to live in. I don't know you and until yesterday I had never heard of you——'

'You've seen me here before.'

'Once, seven years ago. I didn't know your name, what you were doing here. For all I knew you had come to service my father's car . . .' He raised a sardonic brow at that but Fenella wasn't put off. 'Your name never cropped up till last night when my father told me who you were. He said nothing more than your name. You spend a night in my home and then calmly announce you are staying for several months.' Eyes blazing, she shook her head firmly, her hair tumbling around her face in disarray. 'I'm not taking that——'

'What are you afraid of, Fenella?' he questioned lazily. 'Don't you trust me?'

'I don't even know you!' she retorted hotly.

'You know me well enough to know I wouldn't take advantage of you——'

'I know nothing of the sort. You thought nothing of waltzing into my bedroom this morning. I might have been stark naked for all you knew.'

'I knocked, gave you ample time to make yourself decent.'

That was true, though she could argue three seconds was hardly ample time to ensure propriety, although it could have been worse, but then there was this afternoon; *that* couldn't have been worse. She could still feel the sensuality of his lips on hers and the humiliating shame that followed.

'Well, what about this afternoon?' she argued. His jaw muscles tightened but he didn't strike fear into Fenella's heart. 'If that wasn't taking advantage I don't know what was!'

There was a pause before he said anything, a pause in which fear did quicken Fenella's heartbeat. His eyes narrowed murderously and his fists on the desk clenched tightly. 'How you can stand there and insinuate such a thing I'll never know. With your track record I wonder you have the nerve. You came on to me when you were sixteen and this afternoon you were a pushover too.'

How could he be so scathingly cruel? 'You bastard!' Fenella breathed raggedly, tears stabbing painfully under her lids.

'Well, I would be, wouldn't I?' he spiked sarcastically back at her. Then his voice lowered threateningly. 'I'll tell you something, Fenella Trent, if anyone's honour is at stake in this house, it's mine!' With that he turned on his heel and left her standing quivering behind her father's desk.

Exhausted, Fenella slumped back into the chair. She wasn't going to be able to bear it, having this man living in the same house. How dared her father allow it and why, why, why? Maybe all those years ago they had some business connection, but the man had been abroad for seven years and never once had her father mentioned the name of Sam Ballantine in that time. With a sigh of resignation Fenella closed her eyes; so when had her father ever discussed his business with her anyway? All she knew was what she read in the *Financial Times* and the company's annual reports, copies of which were always kept here in the safe at Hunstand Manor. Her father knew she pored over them but he was so sublimely confident his daughter was not going to get a foothold on the board that he indulged her curiosity.

'I'd much rather you buried yourself in one of those women's magazines than those boring old reports,' he'd said one night last winter. They were having a nightcap in the study. The fire was still blazing and Joseph Trent was stretched out in front of it, sprawled in his favourite armchair.

Fenella smiled across at him from the desk where she was going over some of the past reports, a small brandy with her coffee having mellowed her into a good humour.

'These make far more interesting reading,' she murmured, and her father chuckled.

'What's so funny?'

'You. You have the looks of a model and the mind of man, for all the good it will do you.'

Fenella stretched her long limbs like a lazy cat. 'Are you spoiling for a row?'

'Spare me,' he sighed, and she went to his side then, sinking down at the rug by his feet and leaning her head against his knee.

'I'm only trying to take the place of the son you always wanted,' she told him, staring into the red-gold flames of the fire. 'If Mummy had lived you would have had more children, wouldn't you? A son to carry on the family business. I can do that if you'll only give me the chance.'

Joseph Trent chuckled and ruffled her hair. 'I've told you before, the steel industry is no place for a woman, Fenella. They'd eat you alive. The men in the factories want to take their orders from men,

not the boss's daughter who happens to look like
a film star. You'd make me the happiest man alive
if you married well, settled down and had a family.
A couple of grandsons that in my dotage I could
bring into the corporation as my father and grandfather did before me.'

Fenella sighed. 'The suffragettes would turn in
their graves if they heard a statement like that.'

'Don't get me wrong, pet, I'm all for equal rights,
in the right place, which isn't a handful of steel
works in the north of England.'

Fenella hadn't argued any more that night,
because she knew he had a point. On the occasions
she had travelled up to the factories with him she
couldn't help notice the admiring looks, the nudges
and winks, all executed out of sight of her father,
of course. But it had never been her intention to
actually get down on the factory floor as her father
always did on his visits. She could have done her
administering behind closed doors, preferably the
boardroom's closed doors, where her real interests
lay: the economics, the power and the wheeling and
dealing end of Trent Industries.

Settle down, get married, have children? Fenella
shook her head and wandered over to the french
doors. Storm clouds had gathered up the heat of
the day and were ready to disperse it into a deluge
of rain. Already spots were driving hard against the
windows. Domesticity wouldn't be enough for her.
She loved the company she had formed. The money
market exhilarated her. Sam Ballantine exhilarated
her...

Biting her lower lip, Fenella swung away from the window. Why was he here? And then a thought formed and was so ludicrous that she nearly dismissed it with contempt, but she held on to it just long enough for it to make some sense. Hadn't her father said on more occasions than she wished to acknowledge that he wanted her married? Had he set all this up? Invited the good-looking, charismatic Sam Ballantine to stay in his home while he was away on his honeymoon in the hope that he and his daughter might get better acquainted? For some reason Fenella thought that Joseph Trent might approve of Sam Ballantine. He had nerve, for one thing, and her father admired that.

Suddenly Fenella grinned to herself. Nerve he might have but one precious commodity he lacked, and her father wouldn't sell her down the river for nothing. That was precisely what Sam Ballantine had, plenty of nothing! He'd been swanning around the world and was now back in the UK without a car or an evening suit to call his own. And what did he do for a living? She would ask him, of course, not that she was particularly interested, but, whatever it was, it had only afforded him that dismal red-brick cottage with the wild gardens.

No, her father wouldn't do that to her, expect her to fall in love with a penniless nomad. And her father wasn't a gullible old fool ready to fall for a hard luck story either. So how had Sam Ballantine managed to worm his way into the Trent household? Joan! Joan might be able to throw some light on the mystery. A clap of thunder shook the windows as Fenella made her way to the flat she and Dennis occupied above the kitchen and garages.

Joan and Dennis had been with the family since their own wedding-day. Joseph Trent had known both their families in the north before he had bought the manor, offered them jobs when he heard they were getting married and wanted to move down to the south to be nearer Joan's sister.

Although Fenella had had Nanny Parkins till her retirement when Fenella went off to boarding-school, it had been Joan she had fled to when she needed comfort, and comfort she had needed often. Nanny Parkins had been strict, Fenella had been a rebellious child and every day it had seemed there was some minor catastrophe to deal with. Joan had always been there to offer solace and chocolate biscuits. Which was exactly what she was doing now.

Fenella curled up on the dark red Dralon sofa in the cosy sitting-room. Joan made tea in the small kitchen, chattered through the open door about the wedding and how wonderful and happy her father and Adrianna had looked. Fenella wondered why, when she was surrounded by such lovely loving people, her own life was such a mess. True, her professional life was a success, but her personal life lay in shambles. She had little time for friends, always seemed to be working when they were flying off to exotic places for holidays they had scarcely earned. Her girlfriends were the girls she employed and they rarely met outside office hours, and as for men . . . There had always been Simon, of course, but never the closeness they had shared as children and teenagers. Sam Ballantine had ruined that.

Fenella smiled wryly to herself. If only he knew. He was so ready to accuse her of being a seductress that he'd fall over backwards with laughter if he knew her sexual experience amounted to just about nil. Oh, men had taken her out and tried to make love to her, but how could she let them get beyond that first kiss when that first kiss reminded her so cruelly of that hot sultry day in Simon's arms?

'Where's Dennis?' Fenella asked as she took the tea and biscuits Joan offered. Suddenly she was hungry, remembered she hadn't eaten lunch.

'Gone to the pub; he'll get soaked and serves him right.' Joan laughed and sat across from Fenella, nodding to the window where the rain splattered angrily.

Fenella acknowledged the driving rain with a smile that didn't fool Joan.

'What's the problem? It wouldn't be Mr Ballantine, would it? I saw you go off together.'

'Who is he, Joan?' Fenella asked quietly, taking another biscuit and munching on it ruefully.

'Sam . . . Sam Ba——'

'I know his name, Joan, but you know Daddy didn't tell me anything about this. I couldn't believe it when he brought my coffee up this morning and then later, when he asked for a lift, I didn't dream he was coming back here.'

'You didn't know he was going to stay with us till his house is finished?' Joan frowned slightly at that.

Fenella shook her head and levelled her eyes at the housekeeper. 'I don't understand it. You knew, didn't you?'

'Your father told me a few weeks ago when we were discussing the catering arrangements for the wedding. He said Mr Ballantine was a guest and would be staying indefinitely.'

'But why didn't he tell me?' Fenella cried. 'I live here too; I have a right to know who I'll be sharing the breakfast table with.'

Joan poured Fenella another cup of tea. 'I expect your father forgot. What with the wedding and all.'

'I don't believe that. My father runs a huge corporation—he never forgets anything!' Fenella bit out.

Joan passed the tea. 'Don't you like Mr Ballantine, then?' And before Fenella could answer that she bore him no grudge but having him thrust upon her for the duration wasn't her idea of fun, Joan gave out a small laugh. 'Dennis thinks he's quite a character. Remembers when he came here for some business meeting with your father years ago. Parked his old car out front and asked Dennis to fill it up with water as the radiator was about to burn out. In spite of the way he left later that day, he made time to find Dennis and thank him for his help.'

'The way he left? What do you mean?' Fenella asked, her eyes bright with curiosity.

'In a fearful temper, according to Dennis.'

Had she been the reason? Fenella thought with dismay. He had been furious with her and Simon,

probably disgusted, and then after, when she had
flirted with him ... The thought even now brought
a hot flush of shame to her cheeks.

'Apparently your father had thrown him out and
he wasn't too happy about that——'

'Thrown him out!' The terrible thought crossed
her mind that Sam Ballantine had gone back to the
house, reported what he had seen and her father,
choosing to disbelieve it, had told him to leave.

'I don't think I'm betraying any confidences
when I tell you, because your father was so angry
that the whole household heard.'

Fenella uncoiled her long legs and sat up, eyes
clouded with dismay. 'Heard what?'

'The row,' Joan stated firmly, as if Fenella should
know that. 'Of course, I heard nothing. I was too
busy in the kitchen clearing up after your father's
marathon meeting. But Dennis remembers; in fact
we were only laughing about it last night, me,
Dennis and Mr Ballantine——'

'Last night? You were talking about it last night?'
Shame and yet more shame heated her cheeks. Now
everyone in the family knew about her stupid flir-
tation with Sam Ballantine. Would she ever live it
down?

'After the party. You had gone up to bed and
Mr Ballantine was taking a nightcap with us in the
kitchen...' Joan looked pleased at that revelation
and it was quite obvious to Fenella that their latest
house guest had totally bewitched the housekeeper.
Any hope of an ally to help get rid of him would

be a waste of time where Joan and Dennis were concerned.

'I'm so glad it's all blown over and your father and Mr Ballantine are such good friends again. There's more grudges held over money than anything——'

'Money?' Fenella gasped, partly with shock but more with relief. So Sam hadn't let on what he had seen.

'Mr Ballantine can laugh about it now but he said at the time he could have punched your father on his obstinate jaw...' Joan didn't finish because she heard Dennis's car pull up outside the garages and got up to look out of the window.

Fenella got up with her. There was no point in pumping Joan for any more information; better get it straight from the horse's mouth, Sam Ballantine. She was more than curious to find out more about that row and how he and her father were such good friends now.

She ran into Dennis on the back stairs from the kitchen. He was glowing with the driving rain and a few jars of ale. They passed a few pleasantries, mainly covering the success of her father's wedding-day, and Fenella left them to their well-earned day of rest.

Joan had told her there was plenty of food in the fridge but if she and Mr Ballantine wanted a Sunday roast she would come down and oblige. But Fenella had dismissed that idea with a sweep of her hand. She'd reassured her that she was well able to cope for the two of them.

Sam Ballantine came into the kitchen while she was preparing a mixed salad. He looked quizzically at the large amount she was preparing but said nothing. It was Fenella who spoke first.

'Yes, I'm preparing *our* lunch,' she started brittly. 'It seems that I'm stuck with you so the least I can do is make you welcome, for the sake of my father that is. Please don't take this as another ''come on'',' she added sarcastically.

'Learn't your lesson, have you?' He parked himself against the working surface to watch her chop spring onions. Fenella ignored the remark but totted it up on her hate score-board. One more caustic remark to despise him for.

'I hope you've settled in all right and everything is to your satisfaction,' she stated coolly, scooping the onions into the salad bowl.

'The company could be a little less frosty,' he said, picking at an olive in the bowl.

'What do you expect, the red-carpet treatment? I don't want you here but it seems I've no choice. You've bewitched Joan, Dennis thinks you're a jolly decent chap and my father has obviously changed his mind about you since he threw you out of the house all those years ago. I must be the only one who doesn't think the sun shines out of your left ear.'

To her surprise he laughed. 'I wish that I could bewitch you, then truly my life would not be in vain,' he teased, and in a swift movement planted a light kiss on her forehead.

As she widened violet eyes in surprise he turned his attention to the double doors of the American-style fridge. 'White or red wine, or champagne possibly? The choice is yours.'

He could so easily have thrown in a cryptic shot with his question but he hadn't and Fenella thought that if he could keep it up they might just manage to rub along till her father and Adrianna returned to take the pressure off her.

'Red for me. Over there in the wine rack. You're not a vegan or something weird like that, are you? There are eggs and ham going into this salad.'

He laughed. 'One day I'm going to make some lucky woman very happy. I eat absolutely anything but fish stew. So remember, don't ever dish me up *bouillabaisse*.'

She wasn't going to pursue that sweeping statement. The arrogant pig actually believed that the woman who married him would be *lucky*! Poor soul, whoever she might be!

He poured two glasses of Bordeaux and set them down on the breakfast bar. 'I presume you eat here. Hardly worth opening up the banqueting hall just for two.'

Oh, boy, was he getting his feet under the table already. Fenella slammed the bowl of salad down in front of him. 'My father and I always dine at night in the dining-room, regardless of whether we have guests or not, but in his absence——'

'You'd like me to take his place,' he finished for her, helping himself to a liberal plateful of salad.

'But in his absence,' she continued stoically, 'I shall eat out and you can chew cud where ever you please!'

'Cow,' he murmured, taking a chunk of garlic bread.

'I beg your pardon?'

'Cows chew cud, sweetheart, and I rather take exception to being spoken too as if I were some second-class citizen with nothing between his ears but straw.'

His eyes held no amusement now, in fact they shadowed darkly like the clouds outside. His cool statement coincided with an enormous clap of thunder; both sent a shudder through Fenella's body. He was right, of course. This was doing nothing to sweep away the myth he carried about her being a rich spoilt bitch.

'I'm sorry,' she murmured, not raising her eyes from the salad in front of her. 'I have been rude but you seem to have the knack of raising my hackles.'

'Because I'm staying here? I'm sorry if it cramps your style with your men friends but I promise to be discreet and disappear...' His hand snaked out and caught her wrist as she was about to flounce off the bar stool. 'Sit down and eat,' he ordered firmly.

Instead Fenella reached for her wine glass. Any more of this and she could be a raging alcoholic by the time his horrid little cottage was finished. Last night was down to him; she had gulped down champagne as if it had been lemonade, anything to muzz the sight of his face, which had seemed to be gazing down at her from everywhere.

'And I equally resent your innuendoes about my sex-life,' she stated flatly. 'And if you think I'm going to turn a blind eye when you bring someone else's wife here to warm your bed, think again.'

His eyes narrowed. 'I think we ought to call a truce before someone gets hurt, and I don't mean mentally.'

'I wonder who would strike the first blow?' Fenella challenged, lifting her chin defiantly.

He eyed her chin with great temptation. 'It could well be me,' he retaliated sharply. 'You're not the only one with easily raised hackles—you tempt me to knock that supercilious smirk from your face at every insult you aim at me.'

'Insults!' she drawled. 'I thought they were home truths. I do believe you admitted your fluffy bed-mate was someone else's wife. Correct me if I'm wrong.' Forcibly she speared a slice of tomato as if it were his jugular.

'I most certainly will. Your assumption is definitely out of order and I don't recall saying we were bed-mates. Lucy is my brother's wife and I don't bed family.'

Oddly deflated, Fenella swallowed the tomato and took some more wine. 'So how come you take her out——?'

'Dear God, don't you ever give up?' he seethed.

Fenella shrugged, knowing she was pushing him to his limits of endurance. 'She was clinging to your arm like lichen to a tree-trunk. Looked a strange way of playing happy families to me.'

She sensed he was fighting that impulse to land one on her with all of his strength. She took a sideways glance at the muscles of his arms, tautened so stiffly they looked likely to burst.

He ate slowly, measuring the time before he spoke. When he was completely composed he said quietly, 'My brother works on the oil-rigs and is away from home a lot. Lucy doesn't get out very much. If she was clinging to my arm it was because she was nervous. She's not long out of hospital after losing her first baby. She put herself out to pick me up from the airport and I asked her to accompany me to your father's party. She enjoyed it but it was a bit exhausting for her; that's why she left early.'

Neither spoke for a long while. Fenella felt as small and insignificant as a flea. At last she swallowed and spoke in a hesitant whisper. 'I'm sorry for thinking the worst.'

It was all she could offer. It just went to show how first appearances could be so deceptive. She deeply regretted all the derogatory thoughts she had nurtured about poor Lucy. It compared with all the awful things Sam Ballantine had accused her off at their first meeting. Sam had explained about Lucy but there was no way she would get the opening to explain about her behaviour with Simon. Not that she needed to—it wouldn't alter how he felt about her. He thought her a bitch and that was that.

'Would you like coffee?' she asked when he pushed his empty plate away. 'And there's some gateau left over from yesterday.'

He glanced at his watch. 'In a minute. I want to make a call first; talking of Lucy has reminded me to check if she's OK, and my brother is due home tomorrow—I want to know what time to pick him up from the airport.'

And he had no car so no doubt he would ask her to drive him... Fenella bit her lip fiercely and started to load the dishwasher. What was happening to her? She wasn't the spoiled brat he thought but she was rapidly going that way. She resolved to be more charitable in deeds and thoughts. It wasn't going to be easy to suppress the temptation to snap back at him but she would try. If she was sensible about the whole business she could avoid him quite easily. She was out at work all day so their paths needn't cross too often. She frowned. Did he have a job? she wondered. That was one of the questions she had wanted to ask him before this silly word-war had started.

She cut two slices of Black Forest gateau and determined to make her peace.

He took the intention out from under her feet when he came back into the kitchen and sat down at the breakfast bar.

'I've had time to think. If we are going to get on in this house together, all this bickering has to stop.'

'I agree,' she murmured, pouring two scalding coffees.

He raised a teasing brow. 'The lady agrees. Progress indeed.'

'Don't spoil it,' she warned, and he grinned at her.

She raised her dark violet eyes to his and for a fraction of a second his grin wavered. 'I don't want to spoil it,' he told her softly. 'I want harmony. I have work to do and I don't want to waste my wit and sharpness fighting battles with you all the time.'

'That suits me just fine, as I have a business to run as well.' She was relieved he didn't make a cutting remark about a chic little boutique some-where. 'What sort of work do you do?' She wasn't unduly surprised at his reply.

'You could call me a dealer.' He forked gateau and held the fork loosely in his fingers as he waited for her inevitable next question.

'What sort of a dealer?' She had visions of blackjack and casinos but somehow it didn't fit.

'Scrap metal.'

She swallowed a black cherry whole. Second-hand cars. That *did* fit!

'Oh,' she muttered. 'That sounds interesting.' She desperately tried not to sound sarcastic. It seemed to work, for he didn't snap back. It made her braver. 'Can I ask you something personal?'

'So long as it's not too personal.'

'The last time you were here my father threw you out.'

He smiled wryly. 'The first and last time I've been thrown out of anywhere.'

'You were in a fury, apparently.'

'Did your father tell you that?'

'My father has told me nothing about you. I heard it from Joan; she said you were all laughing about it last night after the party.'

'But you don't know why I was so furious?' He lifted his coffee-cup to his lips and watched her over the rim. He didn't look angry or mocking or anything but normal so Fenella relaxed and decided to be open.

'At first I thought you might have been angry with me. Disgusted by what you had seen down by the summer-house, and then me being so ridiculously theatrical and making a pass at you. I was only a kid, I didn't realise what I was doing.' She held his gaze bravely and he seemed to realise the effort that admission must have taken.

He pushed his empty plate away from him. 'You were partly the reason I left in a temper,' he told her quietly. He turned his head to look at her, held her eyes with the intensity of his. 'You were something else unobtainable that day.'

A coil of apprehension tightened inside her. She looked away from him, unable to face the strange softness of his eyes. 'I don't know what you mean.'

'Don't you think I was tempted that day?'

She jerked her head back to him, her mouth slightly parted with surprise. His eyes lingered on her moist lips. He reached out and drew a thumb across their fullness.

'Oh, I was tempted all right, to continue where your boyfriend had left off, but it was all a game to you, wasn't it?'

A game? Oh, no, never a game. She couldn't admit that though. She moved her mouth away from his fingers and lowered her long lashes shyly. Her mouth fizzed with the erotic pressure he had exerted. Just with his thumb he could create havoc with her senses. Her tongue crazed soothingly over the warm flesh.

'Don't do that,' he murmured. 'It has a strange effect on my will-power, weakens it to the point of dissolution.'

'You . . . you said . . .' She took a deep breath to clear her muddled senses. Those words had spun her world. 'You said I was partly the reason you left in a temper.'

Sam Ballantine helped himself to more coffee, breaking the spell he had woven with his last words.

'The main reason was your father's narrow-minded, out-dated, Victorian principles,' he told her bluntly.

Tension arched Fenella's back. He and her father might be good friends now, but obviously they hadn't always been and there was something in his tone that implied he hadn't forgiven.

'I came here seven years ago, among other things, to borrow money from your father . . .' Fenella couldn't help a sharp intake of breath. 'He refused.' He looked at her then, smiled wryly, his eyes deeply penetrating hers.

'And now I'm back, to claim what I expected then and to take up the bonus offer that was thrust on me by a sensuous child who had no idea of the value of what she was offering. I wonder if she does now?' he mused, his eyes challenging her for an answer she was unable to produce.

Her mouth was hot and dry and incapable of coherent movement, but her brain ticked over furiously. So that was why Sam Ballantine was here—for money! And if Fenella Trent was still available he'd take that little offer up too.

Eventually Fenella spoke, summoned a sweet smile to accompany her well-chosen words. 'If my father refused you money then I doubt if seven years would have softened his principles. As for the special offer you've been saving up for, sorry, but it's past its sell-by date. No sale!'

CHAPTER FOUR

THE next morning Fenella woke to the sound of car tyres on wet gravel. Her mind clicked into gear. Simon had said he was coming over for a game of tennis. She hoped rain would lay off play, after the restless night she had just spent tennis was the last thing she wanted this gloomy Bank Holiday morning.

Pulling her robe tightly around her, she parted the curtains to look out of the window. The rain had stopped but the clouds held promise of more. Her room was above the stone-columned entrance and two cars were parked alongside the run of steps to the drive. The first car was a stunning black Jaguar saloon, the second a very ordinary old red Ford.

Two men were standing on the steps of the manor talking to a barefoot Sam Ballantine who looked as if he'd just staggered out of bed. Fenella unashamedly eased open the diamond-leaded window to hear better; she caught the tail-end of a deal and anger stabbed at her.

'Kind of you to bring it round on a Bank Holiday,' Sam said.

'Pleasure to do business with you, Mr Ballantine . . .'

Fenella leapt into jeans and snatched a silk shirt from her wardrobe before powering down the stairs, still doing up the fiddly buttons as she went. No way was Sam Ballantine going to operate his seedy second-hand-car business from Hunstand Manor!

She arrived on the top step in time to see the back of the old red Ford disappear down the drive. The Jaguar was still there, long, sleek and predatory, its new owner dangling the keys proudly from his little finger.

'Beautiful, isn't she?' he breathed.

'But it's brand new!' Fenella gaped at the number plates.

'You know, I could have had one of these shipped out to the Middle East but it didn't seem right somehow. I wanted to wait till I got back to England, savour the moment.' He circled his new acquisition with pride, impervious to the gravel under his bare feet.

Fenella stood as still as stone and watched him in awe. Sam Ballantine wasn't at all what he appeared. With a frown she went inside the house and headed for the kitchen, to grind coffee beans with a vengeance. If he could afford a car like that he didn't need to borrow money from her father, or had he purchased the car on the strength of getting that loan? And as for boasting about having one shipped out to the Middle East . . .

'I thought breakfast in bed was the plan this morning.' He took the coffee percolator from her hand and plugged it in. 'And you've done your shirt up the wrong way.'

Fenella swallowed her anger, remembered her vow of yesterday to keep the peace and turned away from him to rebutton the front of her shirt.

'How modest of you.' He couldn't resist.

She ignored that, but couldn't resist a little dig of her own. 'The second-hand-car business is more lucrative than I thought. That Jag is an expensive car.'

'Second-hand-car business?' He looked at her blankly.

'You...you said...' Suddenly she was very unsure and wished she'd kept quiet. 'I thought . . . you said you dealt . . . scrap metal . . .'

He threw his head back and roared with laughter. 'Oh, darling, you do jump to some odd conclusions.'

'Don't call me darling!' she snapped at him, cross with him for laughing at her and cross with him for reminding her of the 'darling' he had whispered yesterday when she was in the throes of her allergy attack. He could make the word sound an endearment or an insult.

'Sorry, sweetheart, but you are quite priceless.'

'And don't call me sweetheart! I think it was a natural assumption to make. Cars, old cookers, washing machines, they're all scrap, aren't they?'

'Oh, yes,' he agreed, the laughter still brightening his eyes. 'So are old jumbo jets!'

'Jumbo jets!' she breathed incredulously. He must be joking! The phone rang and before Fenella could reach for the wall phone next to the fridge Sam had snatched it up.

'Hello... no, I'm sorry she isn't available. We rather overslept this morning and she's cooking my breakfast at the moment...' His arm came up to protect himself as Fenella lunged at the phone. With the strength of an elephant he held her at arm's length. 'Too wet for tennis? I couldn't agree more, dear boy. No, this afternoon is orf too I'm afraid...' He had Simon's accent off to a T. 'We're going for a drive.' He put down the receiver with a crash, leaving two hands to deal with Fenella, who was nearly apoplectic with rage. He pinned her arms to her side.

'Are you out of your mind?' she screamed at him. 'You led Simon to believe we had spent the night together, and how dare you interfere in my life and how dare you presume I would even dream of coming for a drive with you?'

He held her so tightly that the loss of bloodflow sent pins and needles skittering up her arms. Her violet eyes blazed defiantly like twin amethysts under the predatory gaze of a gem cutter.

His mouth closed over hers, softly at first and then more persuasively as her lips parted as inevitably as a flower tempted open by the morning sun. Her head reeled dizzily as he released his hold on her, slid his arms around her slender body and drew her against him. His body was hot and hard and masculine and she felt as weak and feminine as a woodland sprite in his arms. Her fists slowly uncurled under the power of his kiss but she couldn't raise them to touch him or caress him and she wanted to, how she longed to touch the springiness of his jet hair, to run her fingers down the front of his shirt and slide her hands in to smooth over his chest, but her strength and her will had sapped as if he had drawn it away from her in that one long enraptured kiss.

He eased his mouth from hers, and ran the tip of his tongue along the fullness of her upper lip, raising goose-pimples of sheer ecstasy at the nape of her neck.

'Now tell me who you would rather spend the afternoon with,' he murmured seductively in her ear.

'You conceited swine,' she grated wildly, 'I'd rather play tennis with Simon in a hurricane than spend another second with you!'

His hands slid down her back and he grasped the leanness of her hips and pulled her against him.

Fenella gasped with shock at the reaction of her body as he pressed power-packed muscle against her. It shuddered as if she had been punched and the ache in her loins was so intense that she wanted to cry. He kissed her again, this time leaving no doubt in her mind whom he wanted to spend his time with. It was a kiss as deep and as dangerous as the Atlantic and the tidal wave of desire it raised in her ran wildly out of control. She wanted him then, more desperately than the first time. That need, because of his absence, had been bearable; this need, because he was here, raged through her, running wild and untamable, unstoppable.

Breathlessly she forced herself away from him. 'This isn't going to work ... you in this house ...'

'So you do still want me?' He smiled down at her, still holding on to her.

There really wasn't an answer to that. He wasn't a fool. He must know the effect he had on her. But she was a fool to let her weakness show. Why hadn't she fought off his kisses as she had done with every other man who had come on to her like that? Because he wasn't any other man. He was Sam Ballantine, the fantasy activated into fact.

'I've told you before, I was only a child,' she murmured, lowering her lashes.

'I know that,' he said softly. 'It was one of the reasons I held back.' He lifted her chin to look into her eyes. 'I wanted you that day, Fenella, and I'm not proud to admit that.' She frowned in puzzlement. 'Part of me wanted to take you in anger, to punish your father.'

Fenella's eyes flashed furiously. 'Because he wouldn't lend you money?' She tried to wriggle free of him but he tightened his hold on her waist.

'Yes, but I was also angry with myself for not being able to convince him my ideas were better than his. I was twenty-six and had little experience and your father out-talked me. If I had made love to you it would have been to punish your father and myself. An instant of intense pleasure to be paid for through the rest of my life.'

Fenella's body sagged and he released her. Her eyes burning, she turned to the coffee-pot. 'Would it have been pleasure?' she asked bravely. What more had she got to lose? He'd already smashed what little self-confidence remained after his rejection then. It was absolutely no consolation to know now that he had wanted her. The reasons were too horrendous.

He stood next to her, watching her pour the coffee with trembling fingers. When she put the pot down his hand closed over hers; the other came up to turn her head towards him.

'I think it would have been incredible, and it will be——' His eyes burned with the certainty of it.

'Will be?' she echoed, her heart lurching with fear.

He smiled at the fear blazing in her vivid eyes. 'Inevitable,' he told her smoothly. 'You don't think two beautiful people such as we can live together without temptation taking a hand?'

'You really are the most arrogant man I've ever met,' Fenella seethed breathlessly. 'You're also the stupidest. You think I haven't seen through you? You wanted to punish my father seven years ago but held back because of my age and some peculiar stab of conscience; well, there's nothing to stop you now, is there? Just one thing, dear boy,' she husked sarcastically. 'The lady is no longer willing! The rich spoilt teenager grew up to see through bastards like you!'

'You think I still want to make love to you for revenge on your father?' Sam said coldly.

'Well, don't you?'

'I said part of me wanted you in anger; the other part of me wanted you because you were the most beautiful, desirable creature I had ever seen.'

'Stop it!' Fenella cried wildly. 'Don't think you can flatter me now and I'll fall into your arms.'

'I should hope not. I credit you with more sense.'

'So why say something like that?'

'Because it's the truth. And seven years later you are still the most beautiful and desirable creature I have ever seen and if it's at all possible I want you even more now.'

Fenella gulped at her coffee, scalding her mouth but not caring. She could say those very same words of him. Even standing here next to him in the clinical atmosphere of the kitchen she felt desire tear through her like a blazing inferno. So what was she grizzling about? They both wanted the same thing, didn't they? Each other's body. But she wanted more, had always wanted more in her fantasies.

'Why are you frowning?' he asked.

She couldn't look at him. 'Conflict of emotions,' she admitted in a weak murmur. 'I thought I knew myself but apparently I don't.' She paused for a few seconds, absorbing those new thoughts. All the years she had spent studying, the man with no name had been at her side. She had thought he had been her spur to prove her worth but now she knew it went deeper than that, and the realisation was so disturbing that she didn't want to think about it.

'I think we ought to organise ourselves,' she stated firmly. 'Get one thing sorted out before anything else. I'm not going to bed with you——'

'I haven't asked you yet.'

'You presume it.'

'I know it,' he stated so emphatically that Fenella gave up that line of attack.

'I leave for work at eight every morning and I doubt if I'll be home before that time in the evening——'

'So what are you trying to say?'

Fenella closed her eyes in disbelief. 'If you shut up and listen it will be quite clear.' When she opened them again, he'd moved away to load the toaster, but not before she had seen the corner of his mouth twitch with humour. 'And I don't see what is so funny. I'm just trying to tell you my routine so that in future you will keep out of my way.'

He went to the fridge for butter and though he didn't utter a further word she felt anger nip her as if he had. He was indulging her, that came across loud and clear. But he wasn't going to put her off.

'Make whatever housekeeping arrangements you like with Joan, but be reasonable. I wouldn't want her to suffer too much extra work because you're here. I breakfast at seven-thirty and frankly I'd rather eat alone. What time will you be leaving for work in the mornings?'

He spread his toast liberally with butter and marmalade before answering. 'I wouldn't want to ruin your day, so I'll avoid you like the plague in the mornings and I shan't be going anywhere, apart from checking on the building works and a few trips up north. My work is here.' He bit into his toast and looked at her over it.

'Here?'

'Yes, I have the telephone. It's all I need at the moment so I'll be working from home; that is, my home for the next few months, which happens to be here.'

Narrowing her eyes at him, Fenella said sharply. 'You don't have to sound so smug about it. Whatever induced my father to ask you here I'll never know.'

'Well, he did, and I think it's about time you started to accept it.' He reached for a paper towel and wiped his mouth. 'Your father has given me the freedom of his home for as long as I wish, so I shall eat when, where and what I like and I shall come and go and make as many phone calls as necessary and it will be nothing to do with you whatsoever!' he stated flatly.

'This happens to be my home too!' Fenella protested. Her father had been so unfair to foist this man upon her. He should at least have discussed it with her.

'I know, and I will do everything in my power not to disrupt your routine. I'm sorry, Fenella,' he added softly. 'I realise what you are going through. You're angry with me, angry with your father for not telling you about this arrangement, but it's not my fault. I'll try not to be too much of a nuisance. Look . . .' he glanced at his watch ' . . . why don't you come with me to the airport to meet my brother? It will do you good to get out of the house.'

Fenella saw the offer as a patronising gesture. Her body stiffened and she raised her head proudly. 'I don't want out of the house, thank you, and I'm not interested in meeting your brother if he's anything like you. Besides, there was life before you stepped into this house. I have other plans.'

'Well, don't get too heavily involved. We're still going for that drive later.'

That's what you think, Fenella inwardly decided, as he strode from the kitchen. I'm going nowhere with you!

And it seemed Fenella was going nowhere with any one else that day. She watched Sam Ballantine leave the house from her bedroom window, her heart unwillingly tugging at the sight of him dressed casually in black cords and a soft leather jacket. He was no ordinary man, that was for sure. He circled his new Jaguar before getting in and driving off, obviously delighted with it. It made her consider that she had never experienced such pleasure. All her life she had taken for granted such luxuries; even her own car, bought with her own money, had never afforded her that thrill. She wondered about his background, his family.

With a sigh she picked up the phone by the bed; maybe Simon hadn't yet made alternative arrangements for his day. She looked out of the window. The clouds were still ominously low overhead but it wasn't raining. Perhaps they could have that game of tennis after all.

She put the receiver down halfway through dialling, dragged her fingers through her hair. She didn't want Simon, just as she hadn't wanted him after Sam Ballantine had caught them by the summer-house, just as she hadn't wanted any man since then.

'Damn you!' she breathed into the still air of her bedroom.

The rest of the house was as hushed as her own room. She wandered from room to room downstairs. The less than cosy sitting-room, the vast dining-room, the other two reception-rooms that served no particular purpose but to display Joseph Trent's success. They had all been opened up for the wedding and there had been laughter and noise and fun. Now, there was nothing but the lonely echo of her shoes on the polished parquet between the Persian rugs.

She suddenly missed her father. They had always spent their weekends together, sometimes with house guests and latterly with Adrianna. And that was how it would be when they returned from their honeymoon. Her father and Adrianna. Perhaps it was time for her to move out, find a place of her own.

She settled at last in the study, her favourite room in the whole house. In the winter Dennis lit the fire and after dinner Fenella and her father would retire to its snugness and watch television or play cards or argue or talk. It housed hundreds of books in Regency glass-fronted bookcases and was furnished with comfy velvet armchairs and a chesterfield. The antique mahogany desk that had always been in the Trent family rested in front of the long windows that overlooked green lawns and framed paintings

and photographs of her ancestors adorned the pan-
elled walls.

Would Sam Ballantine furnish his red-brick
cottage with family treasures? Fenella mused, just
a little annoyed that she couldn't get him out of
her mind. It would be interesting to see what he
did with the place.

To try and rid her mind of him she settled to
some work. Opened her briefcase and stared at its
contents till she could stare no longer. She slammed
it shut viciously. This was ridiculous. She needed
air.

Slipping a sweater over her silk shirt, she ran out
of the house, headed down to the river, avoiding
the summer-house. She smiled ruefully to herself.
Thanks to the return of Sam Ballantine she didn't
need its solace any longer. He'd even spoiled that
for her.

Later she returned to the house, tired but more
relaxed after her walk. She ate lunch, alone in the
big kitchen, then went upstairs and showered and
washed her hair. She felt a lot better then and
decided she really ought to get on with some paperwork in preparation for the next day.

She heard the Jaguar rolling back up the drive
later that afternoon and frowned.

'How did you get in and out of the security
gates?' she called out from the study door as he
was sprinting up the stairs to his bedroom.

'Dennis gave me the spare remote control. Good,
I'm glad to see you're ready. I'll just get the keys
and we'll be off.'

'Off—where?' she cried. It was almost as if he'd always lived here.

'I said we were going for a drive. Only to Bramley, I'm afraid, but I do rather need your advice on the house. Slip a jacket on, it looks like rain again.' He flew up the rest of the stairs and disappeared down the corridor.

For a few bemused seconds Fenella stood in the doorway of the study, trying to gather her wits. She thought she'd made it quite clear to Sam Ballantine that she wasn't going for a drive with him and wanted to avoid him in the house at all costs. It was obvious she'd have to reiterate her requests.

'Look, I've got work to do and no time to help you knock that brick hen-house into shape.'

His bedroom door was open and Fenella stopped dead in the doorway. The room looked so completely different from the way it had before. Her schoolfriends had always stayed in this room. It was still furnished the same, of course; traditional antique pine with fabrics of old rose and cream, but once it had always appeared a feminine room. Now it was strewn with very macho paraphernalia. Sam Ballantine wasn't the tidiest person in the world. Jeans were flung over the back of a chair, an assortment of shirts, suits and trousers hung inside and outside of the two free-standing pine wardrobes. The dressing-table in the wide bay window was covered in papers and what looked like rolls of building plans.

'Good grief, Joan is going to have a fit when she sees all this,' Fenella exclaimed.

Sam looked up from a suitcase he was burrowing in. 'Yes, she probably will.' He cast his eyes over the confusion and gave a shrug. 'But you can't swap a lifestyle in two days and not expect some sort of upheaval.'

'You mean you lived in a pigsty when you were abroad?' Fenella parried.

'You can be such a shrew, can't you?' he grated without looking at her. 'Eureka.' He held the keys up triumphantly. 'Come on, sweetheart, get your coat.'

'I've told you, I haven't time——'

'For me, you make time,' he insisted, bundled her out of the room and thrust her into her own. 'I need your help, Fenella. A man can't do these things alone. A woman's touch, especially yours, is very much needed and requested.'

'Don't you mean demanded?' she challenged.

'Call it what you will, but you're coming with me whether you like it or not.'

In a daze Fenella found herself being helped into a red mohair jacket and almost manhandled down the sweeping stairway. They were just going out of the front door when Joan called down the corridor from the kitchen.

'What time would you like dinner tonight, Mr Ballantine?'

'Nine o'clock would be just fine, Joan, thank you.'

'You're unbelievable!' Fenella exclaimed when they were inside the car. 'Anyone would think you owned Hunstand Manor the way you throw your orders around.'

'I did no such thing, simply responded to a simple request.'

Fenella sulkily folded her arms around herself. 'You're taking over,' she grumbled.

He smiled mysteriously at that and Fenella looked at him warily.

'One of the conditions of the offer of your father's home was that I looked after you while he was away.'

'I'm quite capable of looking after my own welfare, thank you very much.'

'I'm sure you are,' was all he said.

The sun came out for the first time that day and Fenella, in her chagrined mood, wondered if he had arranged that as well.

The Jaguar smoothed effortlessly through the country lanes to Bramley. Fenella offered no conversation and nor did he. It was only when they were approaching the rough track that led to the red-brick cottage that a thought occurred to Fenella.

'It didn't take you long to pick up your brother from the airport and drop him home.'

'Timing me, were you?'

'Not at all. I've better things to do than time your comings and goings. It just appears that your brother doesn't live very far away and I'm curious to know why you aren't staying with him instead of causing disruption in my home.'

'Your father wanted me to stay at Hunstand.'

'I can't think why,' Fenella retorted.

'No, at the moment I don't suppose you can. But all will become clear in time.'

Fenella threw him a nervous glance. 'What do you mean by that?'

He shook his dark head. 'Not for me to say.'

'Look, you can't make a statement like that and just leave it in the air.'

'I just did,' he answered, and Fenella knew by the tense line of his lips that he wasn't going to expand on that. 'But to get back to my brother—he is away from home a lot and what precious time he has with Lucy is just that—precious. They haven't been married long. I'd be in the way if I stayed with them.'

'So you're only staying at Hunstand for a month?' Fenella said brightly.

Sam frowned as he swung the car into the narrow track that led to the cottage. 'How do you mean?'

'Well, my father will be home in four weeks' time and he's a newly-wed too. You'll be the proverbial gooseberry then.' Fenella couldn't help a grin of triumph. Let him talk his way out of that.

'So will you, come to that.' He laughed and that wiped the grin off her face. 'Never mind, sweetheart, you can always move in here with me.'

'Hey! You've missed the turning!'

'The cottage?' He carried on down the track that led to Lytton Grange. 'That's the staff cottage, that is when I get round to hiring some help. That's something else you can advise me with. I'm not sure how many staff I'll need to run this place. Well, what do you think of it?'

The Jaguar purred to a halt in front of the Victorian folly that only a rich crank would dream of buying. Fenella sat moulded to her seat, too shocked, too numbed to utter a word. This man was more than a mystery, he was an unfathomable enigma.

The Grange stood solidly before them, over-turreted, over-gargoyled, overgrown. And yet . . .

The sun shone affectionately upon it and in that late afternoon glow it seemed to swell with pride as its new owner got out of the car and stood gazing at it.

Slowly Fenella slid out of the passenger-seat and looked up at the mass of diamond-leaded windows that shone gold and silver in the light. For some inexplicable reason her eyes filled with tears. No one had wanted this house. It was ugly and over-priced and everyone that had viewed it had laughed. Sam wasn't laughing. Pride shone in his eyes.

In that moment Fenella realised how little she knew of this man. This house meant more than just bricks and mortar to him; it seemed that it was a dream realised, a goal achieved. She desperately wanted to know what had been his driving force— and there had been one, deep in his past. Some happening that had spurred him through life to this.

A cold breeze ruffled Fenella's hair and impatiently she clamped her wild hair to her ears so as not to obstruct her view. Sam walked slowly towards the heavily studded front door. As he took the key from the pocket of his leather jacket he turned to her and smiled.

Fenella smiled back and the strangest and oddest sensation ran through her. It was fantasy, of course, easily explained away by the breeze that had whipped up, but it seemed as if when Sam turned the key in the lock the house let out a murmur of relief.

The door opened surprisingly easily and Sam went inside. Fenella waited only a few seconds before stepping towards the house. That odd sensation was with her again, almost a thrill down her spine that she didn't understand. All she knew was that she wanted to be with him in that strange house that murmured in the afternoon sun.

Very softly, she called, 'Sam, wait for me.'

CHAPTER FIVE

'DID you really buy it over the phone?' Fenella asked in a reverential whisper. That was the effect the house had upon her. It was almost churchlike, with as much internal stonework as outside. She was terrified her voice would echo on forever if she raised it.

'It was advertised for so long in *Country Life* that I felt sorry for it and decided to buy it. It has a fascinating history. An eccentric lord built it for the woman he loved, a London socialite. He mortgaged himself to the hilt to pay for it. She hated it on sight, refused to live here with him. He lost his temper and strangled her.' Sam Ballantine turned from the great stone mantelpiece of the huge hallway and smiled at Fenella. 'He entombed her behind that panelling you're standing by...' Fenella shot away from it as if it were on fire. 'He lived here for a few years, went slowly mad and eventually tied a rock around his neck and threw himself in the river.'

'What about the body?' Fenella eyed the panelling as if it were still there.

'It was discovered in the twenties, fifty years after her death. There was a note from the lord telling the world what had happened and a request for her to be buried alongside him.' Sam gave a small laugh.

'The story and the Grange appealed to my romantic nature.'

'I suppose you must have a romantic nature to take a subscription for *Country Life* in the Middle East,' Fenella said in a crass attempt to forget the morbid story.

He laughed. 'It was a form of comforter. I love England and missed everything that was my heritage.'

Fenella sat down on the bottom step of the wide oak stairway. 'If you loved it so much, why did you leave?'

'Your father forced me out when he refused to lend me money. I wanted to start a steel recycling plant. He thought my ideas were too avant-garde. So I went where they weren't ridiculed—abroad.'

'And you've held it against my father ever since,' Fenella stated ruefully.

'On the contrary. Your father did me the greatest of services. Nothing spurs success more than revenge and penury.'

If anyone could understand that, Fenella could. She'd never been broke but revenge had been her spur, to show that arrogant man of seven years ago that she wasn't a worthless spoilt brat. And now he was here, back in her life, and had been doing precisely the same thing to her father, proving Joseph Trent had been wrong and he had been right.

'So, you made your fortune without my father's help, and now you've come back to gloat.'

She watched him running his fingers absently over the dirty stonework of the fireplace. 'Gloating would be wasted on your father; not a trait either of us would be happy with.'

'So why did you come back?'

'Because I'd bought this place and I want to live here.'

It wasn't the answer she wanted to hear, sensing her father was more than involved in his return, but she knew better than to press it. 'So, you made a fortune abroad and now you've come back to England. What are your plans? Start another business?'

'I already have one, Tyne Metals. It's——'

'Tyne Mentals?' Fenella shot to her feet. Tyne Metals was the company that was sparking such interest on the Stock Exchange. Damn, she wished she'd taken more notice at the time.

He raised a mildly quizzical dark brow at her reaction. 'Has your father mentioned it to you?'

'No, he tells me nothing. It's just that....' Fenella's shoulders suddenly slumped. It was time she levelled with Sam Ballantine.

'What's wrong?' Sam asked, coming towards her.

Fenella sank back down to the stair and smiled up at him as he towered over her. She drew the warmth of her mohair jacket around her. It was a chilly house.

'Sit down,' she said, and waited till he'd settled next to her. 'When you arrived I thought you were a penniless nomad but you're not, are you?'

'Gone up in your estimation now, have I?' he asked, not without cynicism.

'I'd be lying if I denied it,' she told him truthfully. 'There's a lot of my father in me. I don't waste time with——'

'With people who aren't rich and successful,' he presupposed, his mouth tightening into that line of defiance she was beginning to be very familiar with.

'I didn't say that, but there is a measure of truth in what you suggest. I doubt very much if my father would have offered you his hospitality if, after your seven years away, you were still begging for money.'

He conceded that point with a nod of his head.

'But that's not what I'm getting at. I had the wrong impression of you when you came, now I know better. I'd just like you to know that I'm not what I appear either.'

He shifted uncomfortably on the stair. 'So you want to tell me about the charities you work for, the good you do for the community. That's what daughters of the wealthy occupy themselves with, isn't it?'

Fenella's anger fizzled but she cooled it with good sense. 'I like to think I'm a caring person and one day, no doubt, I'll get involved in something like that, but I'm only twenty-three and busy with my life at the moment.'

Sam Ballantine stood up then, started to move round the huge entrance hall, examining the damaged oak panelling.

'You're not interested, are you?' Fenella's voice rose, echoed round the room.

He turned and studied her with narrowed smoky eyes. 'You interest me very much.' His voice was loaded with a meaning Fenella was quick to pick up on.

On her feet again, she walked slowly towards him. 'This interests you, doesn't it?' She opened her jacket to reveal her body, like a flasher in a grubby raincoat. 'But what I have in my head doesn't, does it?' He frowned. 'Yes, you may well look puzzled, Sam Ballantine. Good friend of my father's? I can well understand why. You both have the same chauvinistic attitudes towards women.' Her eyes blazed recklessly. 'I work for a living, and not in some poky little boutique you've slotted me into. I have my own money market company, set up out of money from a family trust. OK, so I couldn't have done it without trust money, but I can assure you the struggle to make it work was no different from yours!'

She headed for the front door, angry and bitter. He stopped her as she struggled with the rusty lock.

'Is it through your company you heard of mine?' he asked darkly, pulling her hand from the door.

'Yes, it's raising some interest.'

'Well, don't listen to rumours,' he advised sagely.

Fenella eyed him curiously. Rumours were rife in the money world. 'About to go bust, are you?' she crowed, rather nastily.

He smiled cynically then. 'I wouldn't start that little rumour, if I were you.'

'Are you threatening me?' she said coolly, aware that his hand was still on hers.

'Warning you. I wouldn't like to see my shares plummet like rotten apples off the bough.' His fingers came up inside the sleeve of her jacket and caressed the warm flesh of her wrist. 'Much as I find this conversation fascinating, I would like to get back to the purpose of bringing you here. You see, I don't care if you're mastermind of the decade and have an IQ that would put Einstein to shame; there are some things man cannot do alone.'

Fenella froze, expecting him to lower his lips to hers. The look of disappointment showed in her eyes when he didn't. He laughed softly. 'You women want it all your own way, don't you? You demand your equal rights with a flutter of your delicious eyelashes.'

'Who said anything about equal rights?'

'You did, indirectly. You seem to believe I'll think more of you for knowing you run your own company. I don't and you're right, I'm not interested. Money market, boutique, it's all the same to me. It won't make any difference in bed.'

'You're despicable!' Fenella exclaimed, eyes burning with fury.

'No, truthful, that's all.' His grey eyes sparkled wickedly. 'Now, shall we get on with the house? I'll show you around and you can do what comes naturally to any woman, advise me how to make a home of this place.'

'I'll give you a piece of advice here and now,' she breathed through tight lips. 'Set a match to this dump——'

'Now, now, you know what happens to rich socialites who undermine eccentric lords.' His hand came up and caressed her throat, and the goose-bumps that came up on the back of her arms weren't caused by fear. 'You don't fool me, Fenella,' he said softly. 'I've been watching you. This house had the same effect on you as it had on me when I first saw it.'

'I don't know what you mean,' she husked. She leaned heavily back against the big oak door, all her strength and fight seeming to drain from her.

'Some things are meant to be, right from first sight, aren't they?' He held her eyes with his, willing her to say something.

She didn't answer, couldn't, because she knew it was true. She had known at the first sight of him that he was something special in her life, someone who was meant to be. But he was talking of this strange house, not falling in love.

A gasp caught in Fenella's throat. Falling in love; how had she come to that conclusion? She didn't love him. He infuriated her more than anything. But wasn't that how it all started in those romantic stories she had devoured so hungrily in her teens? But they were fiction and this was life and she was determined not to fall for Sam Ballantine.

'I think you ought to take the advice of a good architect and a team of interior designers,' she managed to say before easing her weight away from the door.

He stepped away from her to let her move from the door and cross the room to the fireplace. He watched her eye the grate mournfully as if she longed to see a blaze of fire bring the place to life.

'I said I wanted to create a home, not a show-piece. That's why I brought you here.' He joined her by the fireplace. 'I want *you* to help me make this place a home.'

She should have said, 'Why me?' but her nerve failed her, sensing that his reply wouldn't be what she wanted to hear anyway not that she was at all sure exactly what that was. As well as infuriating her, he had the knack of confusing her till she didn't know what to think or believe.

'You'll have to do something about heating for a start.' She reluctantly gave in.

He smiled. 'I thought of underfloor heating.'

She raised a jet brow. 'Could be difficult under stone.' She lowered her eyes to the floor. 'And it would be a shame to lose all this history. That lord probably strangled his socialite on this very spot.'

He laughed out loud at that and Fenella's heart twisted painfully. His face lit up when he laughed and he was handsomer than ever, if that was possible. He reached out and took her hand.

'Come on, let's explore. I haven't had a chance to take a proper look around myself yet.'

Still clutching her hand, Sam Ballantine dragged her from room to room till she was breathless. Thankfully the Grange wasn't as big inside as appeared from outside.'

'So, there are six rooms down here,' Fenella stated. They stood once again in the hallway, catching their breath before tackling upstairs. 'And this is the only room with a stone floor, so I reckon you could go for the underfloor heating everywhere else. Kitchen, study, dining-room, sitting-room and what about the room that overlooks the rear terrace? What would you use that for?'

'Kids' room.' He grinned, taking her hand again and urging her up the curving carved oak stairway to the upper floor.

'You . . . you plan on having a family, do you?' she asked, wondering why her heart beat in the pit of her stomach at that thought.

'Of course, that's the whole object of the venture. Marriage, children.' He pushed open the door of the first room off the landing. A fiery sunset stunned them for a moment.

'Remarkable!' Sam breathed, letting go of Fenella's hand to cross the room to the window.

The last burst of indignant sun flamed the diamond-leaded panels of the windows. Sam stood in silhouette, dark and foreboding, as the glass shimmered with orange flame around him.

Fenella stood where he had left her by the door. She clutched her arms around her for comfort. One day he would be standing there with his wife . . . She closed her eyes tightly to blind the image from her mind. She felt cold and desolate and knew she didn't belong here. He had someone in mind for his future. A woman had spurred this purchase, someone he wanted to share the rest of life with, someone he planned on having a family with. And why should that thought tear painfully through her?

She didn't want that sort of life. It went against everything she had fought for all these years.

'Fenella,' he murmured without turning to look at her, 'isn't this the most beautiful room?'

She forced a brittle laugh and said carelessly. 'Yes, I suppose it is.' She turned away and went to look at the rest of the floor, though the interest had gone. Sam didn't join her perusal of the other six rooms and the three bathrooms with their original brass fittings and baths on claw feet.

'What's wrong?' Sam asked, catching her wrist as she was about to sprint downstairs.

'Bored,' Fenella stated flatly. 'We really ought to get back now. I've some phone calls to make and some work to catch up on.'

Was it disappointment she saw cloud his eyes? She turned away and flew down the stairs. No, her imagination again.

She waited by the car while Sam locked up. He took one last look up at the turrets and then turned to walk slowly towards the car.

'You know, it's not in a very bad condition. You could live in it while the builders are . . .' Her voice trailed to a vapour as his eyes iced over her.

They got in the car in silence and drove back to Hunstand Manor in the same way. Fenella left him to put the car away and ran indoors, straight up to her room, where she slammed the door and threw herself on the bed.

She'd upset him and she hadn't meant to and she'd upset herself and what on earth was going on? She pummelled her satin covered pillows in

TAKE FOUR
BEST SELLER ROMANCES
FREE!

♥

Best Sellers are for the true romantic! These stories are our favourite Romance titles re-published by popular demand.

♥

And to introduce to you this superb series, we'll send you four Best Sellers absolutely FREE when you complete and return this card.

♥

We're so confident that you will enjoy Best Sellers that we'll also reserve a subscription for you to the Mills & Boon Reader Service, which means you could enjoy...

♥

Four new novels sent direct to you every two months (before they're available in the shops).

Free postage and packing we pay all the extras.

Free regular Newsletter packed with special offers, competitions, author news and much, much more.

CLAIM YOUR FREE GIFTS OVERLEAF

Mills & Boon FREE BOOKS CERTIFICATE

YES! Please send me my four **FREE** Best Sellers together with my FREE gifts. Please also reserve me a special Reader Service Subscription. If I decide to subscribe, I shall receive four superb Best Sellers every other month for just £6 postage and packing free. If I decide not to subscribe I shall write to you within 10 days. Any **FREE** books and gifts will remain mine to keep. I understand that I am under no obligation whatsoever – I may cancel or suspend my subscription at any time simply by writing to you. *I am over 18 years of age.*

IOAIB

NAME _____

ADDRESS _____

_____ Signature _____

_____ POSTCODE _____

POST TODAY
and we'll send you this cuddly Teddy Bear.

PLUS a free mystery gift!
we all love mysteries, so as well as the FREE books and cuddly Teddy, there's an intriguing mystery gift

MILLS & BOON
FREEPOST
P.O. BOX 236
CROYDON
CR9 9EL

exasperation. Cool it! she ordered herself as she rolled on her back and watched the evening shadows play around the room. He was getting to her, this man who'd already affected her life so strongly. Well, she'd effected her own cure for him before; she could do it again. Work was her panacea.

'Damn!' Fenella breathed as the five-minute dinner gong clanged from the hall. 'Joan,' she called from the study doorway, catching the housekeeper before she disappeared down the corridor, 'I'll eat in the study. I've still got a pile of paperwork to wade through.'

'I don't think Mr Ballantine will like that, Fenella——'

'You're right, Joan, he wouldn't like it at all,' Sam Ballantine said from the bottom of the stairs.

Fenella jerked her head to glower at him, shocked to see he was dressed for dinner and not in the evening suit from the dress-hire company.

'Yes, I do possess my own evening suit,' he informed her cuttingly. 'Joan was kind enough to press it for me this afternoon. Thank you, Joan.'

Joan gave him a beaming smile and swept down to the kitchen.

'I hope you don't intend dining in the jeans you've been wearing all day. I've made the effort. I think you ought to do likewise.' As Fenella's mouth gaped open, Sam Ballantine glanced at his watch. 'You have four minutes to perform a miracle. I'll pour an aperitif while you go for it.' He swept passed into the study and it was all

Fenella could do to stop herself kicking at his shins as he went by.

'I did this for Joan,' she informed him haughtily, four minutes later, when she joined him in the study for a pre-dinner drink.

His grey eyes swept appreciatively over the bronze silk dress she had thrown on in a fever of resentment at being ordered around in her own home.

'Shame. I would have liked to think you had made the effort for me.' He smiled wryly as he handed her a dry martini.

She took it with a sweet smile that quickly dropped from her lips as his hand came up and unclipped the gold clasp that was holding her hair in place on the top of her head. Silky jet hair tumbled in disarray around her shoulders.

'I prefer it like that,' he told her smoothly.

With a defiant toss of her head she shook her layered hair to settle in its own wild way. 'Is that better?' She smiled. 'I suppose it was a bit sophisticated for you,' she said flintily. She drained her martini in one. 'Shall we go and chew cud together?' She took his arm, expecting him to lead the way to the dining-room, but he lowered his lips to hers and claimed her mouth with a kiss loaded with irony.

'I love the bitch in you,' he murmured huskily as he drew his mouth from hers, leaving her as oddly dissatisfied as the enormous gulp of martini had.

'I took the liberty of asking Dennis to light a fire in here,' he told her as they stepped into the elegant gold and pale green dining-room. 'I'm feeling the chill here in England after the heat of the East.'

'Well, we wouldn't want to upset your metabolism, would we?' she offered sarcastically, taking the seat he held for her to his right, not in the least bit surprised when he took her father's chair at the head of the table.

'I also suffer from indigestion brought on by a surfeit of sarcasm. So don't spoil my dinner, will you?'

'My heart burns for you,' Fenella punned wickedly.

She saw the gleam of humour in his eyes over the silver candelabra and relaxed.

Fenella hadn't realised just how hungry she was. The first-course prawns disappeared without effort.

Sam topped up her wine glass. 'I like a woman who isn't picky with her food,' he mused.

Stemming a blush of embarrassment, Fenella smiled. 'It must be all that rushing around that cold house of yours which whipped up my appetite.'

Sam frowned. 'What happened this afternoon, Fenella? You went cold on me.'

She wished she hadn't mentioned the house, but she had, and how could she explain something she didn't understand herself? 'You must admit the house was a bit chilly,' she hedged, taking a gulp of wine she didn't want.

'Don't be evasive; that's not what I meant and you know it. You started to get all enthusiastic about the place and then when we went upstairs you lost interest.'

There was only one way out of this line of questioning and that was a white lie. 'I was tired, actually. The last few weeks with the wedding have been a bit hectic and I knew I had some work to catch up on. It just all got on top of me.'

He seemed to be satisfied with that and then Joan came in with the main course and she was out of trouble.

'Oh, Joan, beef Wellington! My favourite!'

'Mr Ballantine's too. He especially asked for it.' Joan put the dish proudly down on the sideboard and started to slice through the golden flaky pastry and the tender pink meat inside.

Fenella could have made a sarcastic remark about Mr Ballantine's likes and dislikes and the effect he'd already made on the household but she didn't and was glad. Sam gave her a smile across the table that melted her bones to her ankles.

'That was easily the best meal in years,' Sam said with deep satisfaction as he put his knife and fork to rest on the Meissen dinner plate.

Fenella laughed. 'I hope you don't intend poaching Joan from us once you're settled. She's obviously fallen for you but take heed, my father wouldn't part with her for the world.'

'I understand why. She's a fabulous cook.' He stretched back in his seat. 'But I've taken enough already. I wouldn't want to deprive him of his housekeeper as well.'

'As well?' Fenella queried, her eyes narrowing suspiciously.

There was a second of hesitation before he responded with, 'His hospitality. The use of his home.'

Why she should get the impression that there was more mystified her. But didn't the so-called friendship of him and her father mystify her? She wished Thursday would hurry and come so her father could clarify the situation because there was no way Sam Ballantine was going to open up to her.

'Home-made ice-cream or *crème caramel*?' Joan announced as she came back into the dining-room.

'Nothing more for me,' Fenella told her.

'Me, neither, Joan. Thank you for a wonderful meal.' He turned to Fenella. 'Would you like to take coffee in the study?'

Did he know that was the usual routine? He seemed to fit easily into her father's ways. 'Yes, why not?' she said with resignation.

A fire blazed in the grate of the study. Whether or not it had been instructed by Sam or not Fenella didn't ask. She was glad of it, stood in front of the flames and warmed herself. August days had been warm and sunny this year, but the sudden storm and grey clouds had cooled the nights to a wintry chill. She understood how Sam must feel after years in a hot climate.

'I took the liberty of glancing through your work while you were changing for dinner.' He handed her a small brandy.

'You had no right.' She put her drink down on the mantelpiece and crossed to the desk. Her own fault; she should have cleared the papers away before flouncing upstairs to change for dinner. Not very businesslike of her, especially as they were clients' portfolios she was dealing with, strictly confidential. She gathered up the papers and slid them into her briefcase, just a little annoyed with herself.

'I'm impressed,' he told her. 'You have a good set-up there.'

'Yes, it's working out very well.' She took up her brandy and sipped it cautiously. The room was very still and she wished Joan would hurry with the coffee. Something was happening. It was Sam, of course. She sensed that any more evenings like this and they could easily settle into cosy domesticity. Dining, taking coffee and discussing the day's outcome together. He'd shown interest in her work and that was the difference between him and her father. Her father indulged her, listened to what she had to say, but with such a faraway look in his eyes that she wondered if anything was getting through.

'What made you pursue that particular career?' He settled in her father's chair and Fenella sat across from him, kicked off her shoes, wondering what he would say if she replied, 'You'.

'I found I had a flair for it. I was always good at maths and the Stock Exchange fascinated me, and of course the EEC is thrilling and there are so many changes going on in the money markets of the world. It was second choice, though,' she admitted with a small shrug of her elegant shoulders. 'I wanted to join my father's company, still do come to that, but he won't hear of it. Says the steel industry is no place for a woman. His greatest wish is to see me married and producing grandchildren for him.'

He frowned slightly and Fenella noticed but before she could comment he smiled and gazed pensively into the heart of his brandy. 'That's his Geordie origins.'

Surprised, Fenella said. 'You know?'

'We share the same roots, in fact we both originate from the same coal-mining village.' His eyes narrowed for an instant. 'Slightly different backgrounds, of course.'

There was a trace of bitterness in his tone which Fenella picked up on. 'How do you mean?' she asked.

'Your family were well-respected pillars of society. My grandfather was a wanderer, left for Canada. My father was born there but when he grew up he yearned to discover his roots back in England—for all the good it did him,' he added mournfully.

'What do you mean?' she pressed.

He swirled his brandy. 'I was seven, my brother nine, when our father was killed in an accident. Six months later our mother died. Suicide.' He lifted his glass to his lips and downed the brandy in one.

'I'm sorry,' Fenella murmured, looking away from him to the fire. It explained a lot. The pleasure his new car gave him, the folly he had bought to secure him and his children the stability he had lacked in his own childhood. She didn't want to ask how he and his brother had survived the double tragedy, not yet; it was too early, too sensitive an area to broach so early in their relationship. Relationship? Already she was admitting to one.

'Enough of me,' he said quietly. 'You've surprised me. I thought I'd come back to find you either married with a small brood of toddlers or still running wild with the local yuppies.'

'I suppose I should take that as an insult.' She smiled.

'So why aren't you?'

She rolled her brandy glass between her palms. 'This,' she murmured half jokingly. 'Brandy mellows me.' She let out a small sigh. 'Besides, I know you don't mean it. It implies you'd given me some thought over the past years.' She wished she hadn't said that. Brandy not only mellowed her, it put silly words into her mouth.

'Every day of my life,' he said softly, eyes staring into the glow of the fire.

Holding her breath, Fenella gazed at him. One side of his face was shadowed, the other bronzed darkly. Could you trust a face that was so strikingly handsome? Could she believe that he had spared her a thought in the past?

'If that line was meant to melt any reserve I might have towards you, think again.'

He looked at her then, his eyes flecked gold with reflected fire flames. 'I'm sorry you still have reservations about me. You think I didn't mean it?'

Her silky jet lashes fluttered hesitantly at the sincerity of his tone. 'How...how could you...have thought about me?'

'Unwillingly, I assure you,' he admitted gravely and gazed back at the fire. 'It was no pleasure having the image of your naked breasts etched on my mind forever.'

Fenella gave a snort of amusement at that. 'I think I'd prefer to hear that my mind was etched forever on *your* naked breasts!'

He laughed softly. 'You didn't have a mind then, sweetheart.'

'Very true,' she conceded, 'I had a body which you refused...'

'And rightly so.'

'You hurt me,' she admitted jerkily.

'Wounded your pride?' He stood up lazily to pour more brandy and Joan came in with the coffee.

She said nothing, poured the coffees and handed Fenella hers. Fenella looked up at her and Joan gave her one of her knowing smiles before bidding them both goodnight.

She's enjoying this, Fenella mused. She likes Sam Ballantine and she's dying to see what is going to develop between us.

'I'd have done far more damage if I'd taken up your offer and made love to you that afternoon.' He settled back in her father's chair, sipped his coffee thoughtfully.

'If I remember rightly, I only offered you a kiss.'

'And Eve only offered Adam an apple.' He grinned. 'Just a little less self-control on my part and we both might have been doomed. An unwanted pregnancy...'

Fenella threw her dark head back and laughed. 'You sound so quaintly old-fashioned.'

'On the Pill, were you?' His grey eyes shone with humour. 'Of course you weren't, and I don't take my pleasures restricted.'

'Sam!' she giggled, trying to sound affronted. 'I'm sure birth control wasn't the reason you spurned me.' How easily she could talk about it now, even laugh about it.

'You're right. But it would have been a disaster, Fenella,' his eyes darkened seriously. 'We'd have burnt ourselves out in a week; there would have been nothing left of the affair once the fire went out.'

'Would it have gone out?' Fenella asked bravely, aware that his reply might hurt.

He held the helplessness of her violet eyes in the seriousness of his. 'We might have been lucky, but I doubt it. It was too early for us. I had to prove my worth to your father and to myself and you had some helluva lot of growing up to do.'

Fenella leaned her head back against the armchair and closed her eyes. He was right, of course. He'd gone on to make a fortune and because of his rejection she'd made a success of her life, but where did that leave them now? He wanted her, had admitted it and yes, she wanted him, so what was stopping her inviting him up to her bedroom this very minute? To bring to life the fantasies and dreams she had lived with so long? She wasn't afraid to go to bed with him, but she was desperately afraid of the aftermath. She might care too much and he might not care enough.

She opened her eyes and saw him watching her. They both looked away, their gazes paralleling to the dying embers of the fire. She was scared and uncertain and he wasn't helping by being so damned human. Yes, damn him and damn that weird house of his and, more than anything, damn her father for liking him.

'I must go up now,' she told him, slipping her feet into her shoes and standing up. 'The holiday is over and it's back to work tomorrow.'

'Yes. I'll come up with you.' He put the fire-guard in front of the fire and switched off the table-lamps. There was enough light to see their way to the door.

He left her outside her bedroom door after smiling and bending his head down to brush a goodnight kiss on her softly parted lips.

She lay in bed, sleepless with confusion. Tonight they had settled into a relationship that wasn't going to be too hard to bear. Joan liked him and their lives should run smoothly till her father came home. So why couldn't she relax and sleep? Because he was there, in the next room. She'd heard the taps swishing in his bathroom, heard him open his window, heard him move around his room. And then there was a silence which was even more hard to bear. How could he sleep? When her body twisted restlessly under the sheets, that whisper of a kiss still tantalisingly disturbing on her lips. The frustration of it pulsed her nerves with a roaring heat. She had wanted more but he had given her less than less. What sort of game was he playing with her?

CHAPTER SIX

THURSDAY came as a surprise to Fenella. The past two days had flown. Work had been an invigorating pleasure and ... the rest ... It had been nice.

'How's Adrianna?' Fenella laughed, so pleased that her father had phoned her at her office immediately they had returned to Mahé from the islands. 'I bet she's as brown as a nut already. I shall die of envy when I see her. Are you having a marvellous time?'

Her father laughed. 'It's paradise, pet. The most perfect place in the world for a honeymoon. Adrianna sends her love and says Brighton wouldn't have been the same. Now, love, how is everything at home?'

'No problems at all. Joan running everything like clockwork as usual.'

'And Sam, how has he settled?'

'Hmm, Sam,' Fenella breathed on a sigh. 'I'm still mad with you for dumping him on me without a word of warning.'

'You don't sound at all mad.' Joseph Trent chuckled.

'I've got over the initial shock now, but Dad, it was a bit of a dirty trick, you know. You should have told me. You briefed Joan but left me to find out the hard way.'

'It slipped my mind, pet...'

'That's what Sam and Joan said, but I don't believe it for a minute. Listen, Dad...' Her voice took on a more serious tone but the words stuck in her throat. All the doubts and suspicions she had formed about why Sam Ballantine had taken up residence in Hunstand Manor with her father's approval suddenly seemed less important now. 'Oh, it doesn't matter. Just enjoy the rest of your honeymoon.'

'I intend to. I'll give you a call next week.'

Fenella sat for a long while at her desk in her city office. The phone call from her father had said a lot by its omissions. He hadn't asked about her business, not mentioned Trent Industries, had glazed over the subject of Sam Ballantine. She ran fingers through her hair, sweeping it back from her forehead. And why should he? After all, he was on his honeymoon.

She got up and wandered to the window, gazed down at lunchtime crowds surging to the nearest wine-bars and pubs. The Bank Holiday clouds had dispersed and the days were warm and sunny again.

Suddenly she didn't want to be here, in the hot, smoky city. Sam would be at home, having lunch with Joan and Karen in the kitchen. Karen, an impressionable teenager, was as enraptured with Sam as Joan was. Three weeks ago, Karen had threatened to leave and get a job in the new hypermarket that had recently opened on the edge of town; now she was hinting at taking Joan's job over when she retired.

Fenella smiled—and she herself was going soft in the head where Sam Ballantine was concerned. They had played Scrabble till one o'clock this morning and she'd overslept and missed her usual train and hadn't been cross at all.

'Anything urgent on this afternoon, Sarah?' Fenella asked her secretary over the intercom.

'Nothing at all. Oh, that company you asked me to look into—I've got the report here. It makes interesting reading. A very successful and rapid rise to fame. They're buying up every metal works they can get their hands on. Very secure Saudi backing. Shares are going up and I think we should buy immediately before they sky-rocket.'

'Go ahead, and I'll take those reports home with me now. Read them on the train.'

'You're going home now?' Sarah asked in surprise.

'Headache,' was the only reason Fenella was willing to give. It was partly true, spurred on by the confirmation that Tyne Metals was a force to be reckoned with and Sam Ballantine probably one of the richest steel men in the UK.

And she'd thrashed him at Scrabble last night, she mused, gazing dreamily out of the train window at the heat of London shimmering over the roof-tops.

She drove slowly from the railway station to Hunstand. She had a lot to think about, mainly the gentle progress of her relationship with Sam. He'd suggested they spend Saturday and Sunday at the Grange, taking a picnic and going over the folly in more detail and, if the weather kept fine, planning the garden and grounds. Fenella was looking forward to it, looking forward to being with Sam.

Steady, she warned herself. Less than a week she had known him; you couldn't count seven years of fantasy, though he was warming up to the image she had formed of him. A frown creased her brow— not quite, though. The fantasy Sam Ballantine was an impatient lover, the real Sam appeared to be playing a waiting game. After his initial advances to her he had cooled. She knew he felt something; he was kind and considerate and very amusing, but apart from a goodnight kiss *outside* her bedroom door he hadn't attempted to get *inside* it.

She hoped he'd be pleased to see her so early in the afternoon, then wondered if he'd be at the Grange. It was a possibility she considered at the crossroads, then opted to drive straight home and, if Sam wasn't there, to change from her city suit into jeans and join him at the Grange.

Her heart skipped when she saw his Jag parked outside, a nifty white Golf parked alongside it. A visitor? For Sam obviously. Normally she wasn't home at this time.

'Where's Sam?' Fenella asked Joan, who was hovering in the hallway when she breezed in. Fenella was halfway up the stairs before she realised Joan hadn't answered.

She stopped. Joan looked embarrassed. 'Mr Ballantine. He...is...he has a...visitor. They're...outside...somewhere.'

With a shrug Fenella carried on up the stairs, calling out as she went, 'Probably someone to do with the restoration of the Grange. We went through the Yellow Pages last night looking for landscape gardeners.'

'Didn't look like no gardener to me,' Joan muttered out of earshot of Fenella.

She changed quickly into a spicy flame skirt of thin cotton and a matching wrap-over silk shirt, knotting the ends at her waist. Eager to find Sam, she ran down the stairs, her gold bangles chinking lightly.

She found them on the river-bank by the summer-house, the reminder of that hot sultry day so long ago rooting her to the spot. The girl standing with Sam, his arm around her shoulders, the other pointing out across the river, was beautiful. Fenella knew that without seeing her face. She was Titian-haired, Junoesque in stature. She was tanned and healthy and her clothes screamed designer chic. She stood close to Sam, barely a sliver of light between their bodies. Their laughter tore through Fenella's heart like a blunt chainsaw.

Stilling the gold at her wrist with a hand that shook furiously, she turned and fled back to the house before they saw her. She understood Joan's embarrassment now. Since Sam had arrived the housekeeper had monitored Fenella's moods with interest. She'd known her all her life, known Fenella was falling in love with him. And now... Viciously, Fenella hoped Joan would see him for the bastard he was, no different from all those other pleasure-seeking creeps that stalked the earth.

'Oh, I hate you!' she hissed before bursting in the kitchen door.

'Fenny, darling!'

'Simon!' Fenella's eyes blinked in disbelief. He was the last person she expected to see drinking tea with Joan in the kitchen.

Joan looked from one to the other as Simon kissed Fenella affectionately on her cheek and then her eyes widened in dismay as the back door opened yet again and Sam and his visitor walked in.

Hearing the click of the door behind her, Fenella clung on to Simon far longer than was necessary for a greeting of welcome.

'I've missed you, Simon, darling,' she cooed, then jumped back over-dramatically as Sam spoke. If she could have raised a blush she would have done; instead she fluttered her long lashes in false embarrassment. Joan raised her eyes heavenwards and plugged in the kettle.

'Nice to see you again, Simon. Better weather for tennis,' Sam said brightly.

Fenella saw that as outrageous sarcasm and honeyed her voice sweetly. 'And who is this?' Her wide eyes skimmed over Sam's visitor. Yes, she was beautiful, stunningly so. 'My, the Yellow Pages do work wonders, don't they?'

The visitor and Simon were blind to that one, their expressions merely puzzled. Joan pursed her lips and Sam's eyes narrowed murderously.

Sam covered the insult admirably. 'Fenella and I were going through the Yellow Pages last night, looking for an interior designer...' Fenella mouthed 'gardener' for Sam's eyes only. 'Fenella is obviously under the misapprehension that Mercedes is the one we agreed on. She is in fact my UK secretary. She brought me some papers to sign.'

Mercedes! UK secretary! Fenella was speechless, Joan relieved and Simon stricken.

'Mercedes!' he enthused. 'An incredible name for a simply incredible lady.' His hand shot out in greeting. 'Simon Taylor-Parkes, delighted to meet you.'

'My pleasure, I'm sure,' Mercedes drawled in such a heavy American accent that Fenella's heart sank like the *Titanic*. Sam had obviously known her since his years in the States.

Reading her mind, Sam volunteered, 'Mercedes worked for me in America. She was such an excellent secretary that when I set up over here I sent for her.'

'Can't say I blame you.' Simon grinned, his pale blue eyes eating up the stunning American beauty. 'If I thought I could get a secretary like you, Mercedes, I'd seriously contemplate getting a job.'

Even Fenella laughed at that. For a moment the tension was eased and cups of tea were passed around.

Simon was enthralled with Mercedes and any notions Fenella had nurtured of using Simon to make Sam jealous were squashed. Simon only had eyes for Mercedes; he was eagerly trying to impress her with tales of his year in the Caribbean but, sadly for Simon, Mercedes's golden eyes never veered far from Sam's amused features.

'Will there be four for dinner tonight?' Joan asked Fenella when the others had stepped outside to the patio to make the most of the good weather.

'No way!' Fenella shot bitterly, helping her with the dirty teacups.

'Just the three of you then?'

Fenella swung to her. 'What do you mean, the three of us?'

Joan refused to look her in the eye. 'Mr Ballantine has invited the young lady to dinner.'

'He's done what?' Fenella exploded. 'How dare he? How dare he?' She went to rush for the back door, to give Sam Ballantine a piece of her mind.

'I wouldn't if I were you, Fenella,' Joan said quietly, but forcibly enough to catch Fenella in her tracks. 'It will show that you mind and, after all, she is only his secretary.'

Fenella gazed at her stupefied. 'Do you believe that?'

Joan shrugged her shoulders, and lifted a lock of silvery hair from her brow. 'It's not for me to say, but if I were you I'd prefer to give him the benefit of the doubt before I go making a fool of myself.'

'When I want your opinion, Joan, I'll ask for it!' Fenella stormed, her cheeks flushed with rage.

'Suit yourself,' Joan told her calmly, not at all offended by Fenella's outburst. 'But, all the same, a foursome is better than an awkward threesome.

I'm sure Simon would only be too happy to make up the numbers.'

'Then there would be the two of them drooling over her,' Fenella bit out, not at all placated by the housekeeper's conciliatory suggestion. She flung down the tea-towel she had been wringing in her hands. 'Do what you like. My opinion isn't worth anything in this house lately.'

She stormed out of the double doors and ran up to her room, changed quickly and furiously into her bikini, wishing she hadn't come home so early. She slipped a towelling robe round her shoulders and hugged it to her. But what difference did it make? That girl would still have been here... If there was nothing to hide and she was his secretary, why hadn't he told her she was coming? Guilty conscience, that was why.

The river was calm but cold and Fenella felt the chill as deeply as she had felt the pain of catching Sam with another woman. She struck out from the river-bank, swimming feverishly to warm herself. She heard Sam's shout as cramp gripped her left calf.

'You idiot, there's a strong current out there...'

Fenella had already turned to thrash her way back, kicking out her right leg strongly. Sam hauled her up to her feet as she reached shallow water.

'Let go of me!' she cried, pushing him away, limping to the grass and at the same time frantically trying to massage the life back into her leg. 'I know this river better than you.'

'So how come you didn't see that swirl out there? You were heading straight for it,' he blazed, flapping his wet shirt away from his chest where she had soaked it.

'I'm a strong swimmer...'

'Looks like it! Cramp?'

Fenella collapsed on the grass at his feet and rubbed feverishly at the knotted muscle. 'No, water on the knee!' she snapped sarcastically.

'Here, let me have a go at it.' He dropped to his knees and took her leg. She kicked at him furiously but he held on. 'Temper, temper! Now keep still like a good girl.'

'I'm not your good girl... Ouch...you're hurting!'

It was over in a second—his hands manipulated the muscle out of its spasm and the relief had her uttering a cry of torment and collapsing back on to the springy grass.

Her eyes, closed tightly against the sun, didn't see him lower his head. His mouth on hers was a shock, his lips persuading hers apart with experience and a deathly resolve to have their way. Fenella's heart spasmed and then every muscle tautened as if her whole body was about to cramp. Strength erupted and she toppled him away from her. She scrabbled to her feet.

'How dare you do that...?'

'I dare!' he raged, lunging at her ankles, bringing her tumbling down next to him.

Winded, she gasped for breath as he rolled her over on to her back and straddled her, pinning her flailing arms above her head. He towered over her, grey eyes nearly black with anger, mouth severe and threatening.

'Is...is this...the only way you can get a woman...' she wriggled under him hopelessly '...by force?'

'Would I be forcing you?' he challenged blackly.

'You...bet! Now get off me before I start screaming for help.'

'No one would hear you.' He laughed cynically. 'And how very fitting if I took you here, on this grassy slope where it all began.'

'Huh! The roles are reversed now, Sam Ballantine. *I'm* rejecting *you*!'

'You're rejecting nothing, sweetheart, because nothing has been offered. I was making an observation, not stating an intention.'

Boiling with rage, Fenella struggled even more feverishly, but it was hopeless. 'So what's all this about if it's not rape?'

'It's about finding out why you are such a rude, arrogant, spoilt wretch who sees fit to insult strangers.'

'What the hell are you getting at?'

'Mercedes.'

'Mercedes,' Fenella mimicked. 'What sort of name is that? Runs on all four cylinders, does she?'

He released her then, not in anger but in laughter. He sat beside her, arms clutched around his knees, and laughed.

Fenella sat up, rubbed her wrists where he had held her so tightly and glowered at him.

'I don't see what's so funny,' she muttered.

He turned to her, eyes glinting with mirth. 'You're jealous, aren't you? That's what your little display of bad manners was all about. You think Mercedes and I are having an affair.'

Fenella blushed crimson to her roots. If she denied it she would look a bigger fool because it was all so obvious.

'Does that explain why you are so rude to Simon?' she retaliated sharply.

'I don't see Simon as a threat, just an irritating nuisance.'

'He happens to be a good friend of mine. We practically grew up together. As a guest in my father's house you have no right to insult my friends.'

'But it's all right for you to insult my secretary?'

'This isn't getting us anywhere,' Fenella huffed impatiently.

'What do you want, an apology for being rude to Simon?'

'Forget it! I'm not bargaining apologies.'

'No, you're too damned ignorant for that!'

'Me, ignorant?' she husked, struggling to her feet. He rose with her, stood so arrogantly close that she unwillingly inhaled his cologne, musky and exclusive. She stepped back. 'You could do with a few lessons in manners. Ever since you came here you have ridden roughshod over the whole household.'

'I've done nothing of the sort,' he told her calmly. 'If Joan asks me what I would like for dinner I tell her. I'm sorry if you think my request for a fire in the dining-room is out of order. In future, I'll put on a vest!' He turned away from her, stepped over her towelling robe and started to walk away.

'And . . . and what about the Texan Torso?' she called after him. 'I come home from work early and find her here, unannounced, and you expect Joan to cook for her . . .'

Without turning he called back, 'I'll ask her to leave.'

'Sam!' she called hysterically. He stopped then, swivelled slowly to face her. 'I'm . . . I'm sorry,' she said flatly, lowering her lashes self-consciously. 'Don't do that; don't make me feel bad.'

When she raised her head he was standing in front of her, tall, handsome, disturbing. Was it any wonder jealousy had knifed her when she had seen them standing so intimately together.

'Do you want her to stay?' he asked, running the backs of his fingers down her arms.

Her eyes were more violet than ever as she looked up at him. She nodded her head vigorously and he laughed softly.

'Liar,' he murmured, and kissed her soft lips. 'Now tell me the truth, are you jealous of her?'

She couldn't answer. Her throat constricted nervously. To make such an admission was equal to telling him she loved him.

'Will it make it any easier for you if I tell you my blood froths when Simon's name is mentioned, that seven years ago I could have committed murder on this spot because he was on the verge of making love to you?'

Her strength went then, her shoulders sagged limply as the blood drained from her limbs. What was he saying? That he loved her?

'So...so you're jealous and I'm jealous...where does that leave us?' she whispered.

'In a very interesting position indeed,' he told her softly, before lifting her chin and claiming her mouth in an impassioned contact that sizzled every nerve-ending in her body. She linked her arms around his neck, stroked the black silkiness of his hair as their kiss deepened. This was what had spurred her all these years: she'd *known* one day he would be back for her.

His hands caressed her shoulders, grazed down the front of her, gingerly plucked at the wet bikini fused to her chill body.

'You're cold,' he murmured. The sun was low now and Fenella shivered. 'Hold still, I'll warm you.' He peeled the wet bikini from her skin, the top first, casting it carelessly aside. Her nipples, already hardened by the cold, warmed silkily in his mouth. She moaned softly, closed her eyes ecstatically.

Sam reached down and lifted her robe from the ground, draped it round her shoulders. Under cover of the soft towelling he knelt and eased the lower half of her bikini from her hips. He nestled his mouth into the soft triangle of hair, cupped his warm hands around her bottom and pulled her against him. Fenella reeled with the impact of white heat that raged between her thighs. He sensed her pleasurable shock and eased his mouth away with soft kisses. He lay his cheek against the flat chilled flesh of her stomach, warming life back into her.

'Sam,' she murmured throatily, her body tense, hot and cold at the same time, her fingers raking tremulously through his hair.

'I know,' he grated emotionally. Straightening up, he folded her into his arms. 'Not here, my darling,' he whispered in her hair.

Slowly they made their way back to the house, were greeted by Joan in the hallway. Her eyes flicked to each of them and then the wet bikini dangling from Sam's fingers. She smiled.

'You may or may not be pleased to hear there will only be two for dinner tonight. Simon has whisked Mercedes into London, a film and supper after at Langan's.' To Sam she directed, 'She said she'll phone first thing in the morning and not to forget to read and sign those contracts.' She bustled off in the direction of the kitchen and Fenella and Sam turned to each other and burst out laughing.

Sam hugged her close. 'You witch, you willed that to happen, didn't you?'

'Didn't you?' she laughed. Before he could agree the phone rang and he went to it. It was his brother and Fenella left him and ran upstairs to shower, happier than she had ever been in her life.

After showering quickly, Fenella slid into baggy jeans and a Benetton sweatshirt. It was too early to dress for dinner. If Sam wasn't too busy there would be time to go over the building plans for the improvements to Lytton Grange. Already the roof was being retiled, in old tiles salvaged from a derelict building of the same period. The local builder Sam had hired was proving to be a wonder. He knew several specialist stonemasons and carpenters and estimates were already filtering in.

Fenella made coffee before joining Sam in the study where he was working.

He looked up when she came in, frowned for an instant and then smiled and stood up to help her with the tray of coffee and biscuits.

'My brother, Andrew, and Lucy want to come over to the Grange at the weekend. Do you mind?' He set the tray down on a pile of papers on the desk.

'Careful.'

'It's all right, they're not important,' he told her hastily. 'Do you mind if they come?' he repeated.

Fenella poured two coffees and laughed lightly. 'It's your house, why should I object?'

'Well, we planned on having a picnic there and two's company...'

'And four's not a problem if it's your brother and his wife.' She smiled. She took her coffee and wandered over to the window-seat. She liked the feeling of being involved with his family. She wanted to meet his brother and was looking forward to meeting Lucy, properly this time. 'I'll ask Joan to pack extra food. It will be fun.' She looked across at Sam, but was disturbed to see him distracted, fiddling with a pen on the desk, letting his coffee go cold.

She stood up and went over to him. 'I'm sorry, I've disturbed your work, haven't I? I'll clear this stuff away and let you get on.' She bent and lightly brushed a kiss over the top of his head, thought his fists had clenched on the desk as she did so, knew for certain they had when she lifted the tray from the pile of papers.

The tray, biscuits and coffee-pot fell to the floor with a crash. Fenella stared, wide-eyed, mystified, and then her eyes blurred with rage at the sight of Trent Industries' annual reports exposed from under the tray.

Immediately her eyes flew to the safe, a heavy floor model wedged between two bookcases, where her father kept all his business papers. Her heart twisted agonisingly. The door was slightly ajar.

'What the hell do you think you're doing?' she fumed, eyes searching his face wildly. 'How——?'

'Fenella, I can explain.' His expression was regretful and Fenella struggled with the urge to slap it from his face. He wasn't sorry for spying, but sorry he'd been caught!

'I'm sure you can! I'm sure you have some slick, well-rehearsed excuse for your despicable behaviour but I don't want to hear it——'

'Listen to me, Fenella!' he roared, his temper so quick to erupt.

'I won't! Because nothing you can say will satisfy me,' she cried angrily. 'You're clever, you eased your way into my father's confidence, but you didn't fool me. I knew, I just *knew* there was more to all this . . . you staying here at Hunstand.'

'Your father invited me——' he choked, battling to hold his temper, a muscle at his jaw vibrating so madly that she knew how hard he was struggling to hold back.

'My father must have had a brainstorm! Just wait till I tell him you've been rifling through his reports——'

'He knows!'

Fenella shook her head from side to side. 'Like hell he knows! Don't try and pull that one on me. I'm sick to death of hearing what good friends you are. I don't believe it, not one word——'

Sam stepped towards her, dangerously, cutting the words from her lips as if he had struck her. 'Believe me, Fenella. Your father gave me his full permission to go over those reports. How do you think I knew the combination of his safe?'

'Huh! I wouldn't put it past you to have done a course in safe-breaking before you came here!' Furiously she lunged for the phone. 'I'm going to clear this up, once and for all. I'll call my father——'

'You'll do nothing of the sort!' He snatched the phone from her hand, slammed it out of her reach.

'Now I know for sure you are trying to hide something. You're terrified my father will come tearing back from his honeymoon and expose you for the traitor you are!' she blazed, her cheeks burning with anger.

Sam Ballantine raked a furious hand through his hair. 'That is precisely what I'm trying to prevent. I don't want your father rushing back just because his hysterical daughter won't listen to reason. Don't be such a spoilt, selfish child, Fenella. Your father is on his honeymoon. Do you want to ruin it for him?'

'I'm sure he would thank me for it——'

'He wouldn't!' He glowered at her, then his shoulders sagged in exhaustion. 'Look, this is ridiculous. I have work to do and this really isn't my problem. It's yours and your father's.' He turned his back on her.

'What . . . how do you mean?'

He turned back to her, his eyes cold and expressionless. 'Why don't you prove to your father and to me how smart, businesslike and co-operative you can be and show a little patience? When he returns I'm sure he'll explain everything to you, but trust him and trust me.'

'How can I trust you? You've taken over my home, I find you going through my father's papers. What am I to think and believe?' she cried plaintively.

'I'm not at all surprised your father won't allow you in the company,' he told her coldly. 'You're typically feminine, won't listen to reason, scream when you can't get your own way——'

'You make me that way!' she retorted. 'I don't run *my* business like that. It's you! You won't tell me what's going on!'

'I *can't* tell you. I'd be betraying a confidence and you can insult and push me to the brink of murder but I won't tell you anything more than you already know, and that is that your father has allowed me to live in his home and to go through his company reports. I wish with all my heart that you hadn't found me working on them, but you have, and I'm sorry the only explanation I am free to give is that I have your father's full blessing.'

'You won't tell me why?' she murmured, all anger abated inside her.

'No, I won't.'

The statement came flat and final and she knew she would get nothing more from him. She bent down and gathered up the shattered pieces of Meissen. She said nothing as she lifted the tray. Sam came round the side of the desk to open the door for her. Neither spoke a word as he closed the door behind her.

The soft click of the catch seemed to echo a death knell around the hallway. A short time ago she had been so happy; now her heart lay heavy in her breast. He'd asked her to trust her father and himself. To trust her father came naturally; to trust Sam Ballantine would take a strength of will she knew she didn't possess.

CHAPTER SEVEN

'I THINK you are being extremely childish,' Sam told her at the weekend.

Fenella had been avoiding him, but come Sunday morning he had cornered her on the gallery landing and, with his arms on the wall each side of her head, refused to let her pass till she agreed to come to the Grange to meet his brother and sister-in-law.

'I must be if you keep telling me I am.'

'You are,' Sam insisted. 'You've locked yourself away in your room——'

'I've been working.' That was no exaggeration. There had been a flood of new clients by recommendation from existing clients and new portfolios were being set up. Fenella had thrown herself into it feverishly. On Saturday she'd worked in her bedroom to keep out of his way.

'No one works on a Sunday, Fenella, so relax and let's have that picnic at the Grange as we planned.'

'It's different now.' She wouldn't look at him, stared blindly at the rich burgundy carpet at her feet.

He lifted her chin. 'Because of our row?' She didn't answer. 'Because you didn't get your own way?' She didn't answer. 'Have your feelings changed for me?'

Her violet eyes hardened defensively. 'Did I have any feelings?' she uttered miserably. The days avoiding him had been bleak. It was all right when she was working—just—but the second she lost concentration Sam Ballantine slid into her conscience to drive her insane with doubts.

'I thought so. Down by the river-bank we came to some sort of appeasement, recognised our feelings for each other, didn't we?'

'And then you spoiled it.'

'By not divulging a confidence between your father and me?'

'It hurts me to think neither of you trusts me enough to let me know what is going on,' she bleated plaintively. 'I know my father's business. If there was something you wanted to know, I could tell you; you don't need to delve into all those old documents. I don't even know why you're doing it. Is my father helping you set up another company? Are you going to work for him? Why don't you *tell* me?'

His hands dropped from the wall to her shoulders. His hold was gentle and compassionate. 'Fenella, sweetheart, it's not for me to say. I told you before, you must talk to your father when he comes home.'

Maybe she was being a little unfair blaming Sam for everything. Her father was definitely keeping something from her. He never would discuss business with her and all she knew was what she found out for herself. It had occurred to her that as Sam was buying up companies he might be trying to persuade her father to part with some of Trent Industries. She'd dismissed that thought because of the sheer magnitude of her father's corporation. Not even Sam Ballantine could contemplate that!

'And do you think he'll tell me what is going on?' Fenella asked.

Sam's eyes darkened. 'He'd better. I can't bear to see you upset this way. I know you love your father, Fenella, but he can be an infuriating man. Obstinate——'

'You don't need to tell me,' Fenella interrupted, her mouth grim. She drew herself up proudly. She didn't want Sam to see just how deeply her father had hurt her, now or in the past. Not to have told her Sam Ballantine was going to live at Hunstand Manor was enough, but this latest development was unforgivable.

'I think it's best we try and forget it till he gets back,' she murmured. It would be hard but she had to try. This rift between them was almost unbearable and her work was going to suffer if she nurtured this anger inside her. She smiled. 'You're right, it's Sunday and the weather is holding, so let's make the most of it.'

His smile was worth the effort of trying to forget her father, Trent Industries and Tyne Metals. His hand smoothed down her cheek. 'That's better,' he soothed, 'we both need a break. Let's not upset Joan any more——'

'Joan?' Fenella looked puzzled.

'Don't tell me you haven't noticed her long face lately? She hates to see us at odds with each other.'

Fenella laughed lightly. 'Let's make her day, then, and sort out the picnic.'

They went downstairs together, hand in hand, and Joan's smile was another that convinced Fenella she was doing the right thing, putting the mystery of Joseph Trent and Sam Ballantine behind her.

'Oh, it's so cold in here!' Fenella exclaimed, pulling her jacket around her, glad she'd worn jeans but sorry she hadn't brought a thick sweater to go over her thin lacy blouse. 'I think we'll have the picnic outside in the sunshine.'

'No way!' Sam laughed, dumping the picnic hamper and the cold box down in the hallway. 'I want to celebrate, here in my new house.' He pulled her into his arms. 'Come here, I'll soon warm you.'

His kiss did just that, made her glow with such warmth that it was as if a fire blazed in her heart. She held him tightly, lovingly, wanting this feeling of belonging to last forever.

How strange she should feel that way, as if she belonged to him. The last time she had been here she was convinced he had someone else in his heart; now she hoped it might be her. And it was a strong possibility that she was. He could have made love to her on the river-bank but he hadn't, he'd shown a restraint that proved it wasn't just her body he craved. There was more, much more, there had to be.

'Feel better now?' he murmured in her hair.

'Warm as toast,' she told him contentedly.

'Good. Now I'll warm you even more. Outside,' he ordered lightly, 'we have work to do.'

She pushed him away from her with a laugh. 'If you think I'm going to pull weeds with you, think again. You'll need a team of gardeners to tackle that lot.'

'Nothing of the kind.' He smiled down at her. 'The gardeners move in next week but you want your picnic in style, don't you?' He laughed at the widening of her lovely eyes. 'We can't have a picnic without a fire, so we're going to gather wood and start the biggest blaze that fireplace has ever seen.'

They spent an hour outside in the grounds, gathering wood and getting side-tracked every time they found something new. A walled vegetable garden, thick with nettles and clogged with ivy. An ancient greenhouse with an old vine valiantly twining its way to freedom through a broken pane in the roof. There were stone statues of Greek gods, broken and lichen-green, a sadly neglected pond choked with lilies, amazingly still flowering.

'What a paradise!' Sam breathed, and Fenella laughed, thinking of the pristine grounds of her own home. She'd taken its beauty for granted all these years. Sam was making her see everything in a new light, or was love sharpening her vision the way it had done seven years ago?

Their arms laden with broken boughs and twigs, they struggled back to the house in time to see a car draw up in front of the Grange.

'They've brought the dogs with them,' Sam commented with concern. 'You're not allergic to dogs as well, are you?'

'No, only cats,' she laughed, struggling to keep up with him as he strode to greet his brother, Lucy, and two border collies who were happily tearing around the gravelled drive.

'Good,' he said quietly, 'we'll have a few when we're settled.'

Fenella's pulse raced at those words. We, as if she was a part of his future. There was no time to ponder on the thought, but happily she stored it away for later.

Sam made the introductions and Andrew, as dark and as attractive as his younger brother but smaller and stockier in stature, relieved Fenella of her load of wood and leaned forward to kiss her lightly on the cheek. Fenella was pleased that he felt relaxed enough with her to make the gesture.

'We didn't get the chance to meet at your father's wedding,' Lucy said shyly as they went inside the house. 'It . . . it was a bad time for me.'

'I'm sorry,' Fenella said gently. 'Sam told me. I hope you're feeling better now.' She looked better, not quite so fragile as before. She was extremely pretty, very doll-like, the sort of woman men ached to cherish and protect. Though dressed casually in tight jeans and a baggy lemon sweatshirt, she came across as very feminine and vulnerable.

'Now Andy is home, everything will be all right.' She smiled at Fenella and then gazed in wonderment at the house.

'What do you think, Lucy?' Sam asked her, heaving the wood down on to the stone floor by the fire. Andy did likewise with his load.

'I ... I don't know what to say,' she breathed hesitantly, gazing up at the massive stairway, the patchy panelling and the chipped stonework. 'It ... it's strange ...' she spun on her tiny heels, '... but ... yes ... yes, I like it very much.'

Fenella smiled and Sam breathed an exaggerated sigh of relief. 'That makes four of us with more money than sense,' he joked.

'You speak for yourself.' Andy laughed. 'I haven't told you what I think of it yet.'

Sam gave Fenella a look of long-suffering and linked his arm possessively around her shoulders.

Andy strode around the great hallway, keeping them all in suspense with groans and sighs as he tapped the faulty panelling, hearing the dull sound of dry rot, scraped the heel of his boot along chipped and crumbling flagstones.

'If nothing else, it has potential,' he said at last, and gave a deep sigh. 'But I'll say one thing for my brother, when he wants something he goes for it ...'

'Enough of that,' Sam groaned. 'Do you like it or not? Not that your opinion is worth a jot ...'

'OK, OK. I like it!' Andy grinned. 'But tell me, is it a dry house or what? We've been here all of a minute and no one has offered us a drink yet!'

And that was how it was for the next half-hour, fun. Sam opened a bottle of champagne from the cold-box and they toasted the house and the future with paper cups brimming with sparkling champagne and then they examined every room, all vying to give their opinion, making jokes and laughing.

Then Sam suggested they light the fire and Andy and Lucy went downstairs, Andy to fetch rugs from the car to sit on and Lucy to check to see the dogs weren't getting into trouble. Fenella stood with Sam in the room where the sunset had framed him in molten gold.

She took his hand as they gazed out of the window. Clouds were gathering again and a wind getting up. A few prematurely bronzed leaves from a plane tree outside fluttered down to the mossy terrace below.

'This house means a lot to you, doesn't it?' she said softly.

He gripped her hand tightly. 'It will be my first real home. Andy and I grew up in orphanages, three to be precise. We weren't easy kids to care for. The authorities moved us on when we got difficult. Andy had a temper. Thought with his fists before his head.'

'And you?'

'Oh, I had a temper too, but I was more of a thinker than Andy. I shelved my anger and bitterness, challenged it into my work. I made plans, not all successful. I learnt the hard way but I learnt . . .' He stopped, turned her into his arms to face him. 'Fenella . . .' his eyes were seriously grey, giving Fenella an odd sensation of disquiet inside her '. . . Fenella, I'd never do anything to hurt you, whatever happens, believe that of me.'

She frowned. 'What do you mean——?'

There was a shout from Andy downstairs and Sam stiffened against her, momentarily tightened his grip on her as if he never wanted to let her go. Then he released her when Andy called out again.

'I've taken the liberty of lighting the fire,' he yelled. 'So what about this picnic you dragged me out for?'

With a resigned smile Fenella crossed the room to the door. Sam called softly to her when she reached it, and she turned, framed in the doorway.

'You know this house is for us, don't you?' he husked.

Tears blinded her eyes and her lashes lowered to stem them. Of course she knew, she had known the first day when the house had murmured its contentment. She wanted to tell him that, and that she knew they had been destined from the first day they had met. It was what all those seven years apart had been about. The waiting time, the growing time. And she would tell him, later, when they were alone. For the moment she just whispered, 'Yes, Sam. I know.'

A fire crackled brightly in the big grate. Andy had brought rugs and cushions from the car and Lucy was arranging them in front of the stone fireplace. She looked up as Fenella came down the stairs.

'Fenella, it's starting to rain. Is...is it all right if the dogs...?'

'Oh, Lucy, bring them in, of course.' She looked up from the picnic hamper as Sam came down to

join them. He smiled at her across the confusion
as the dogs, yelping with excitement, flung themselves on the rugs and took up the best positions
in front of the fire, but there was something behind
the smile that she didn't understand.

Joan had packed cold chicken and pasties and
fresh salad in a bowl, creamy potato salad in
another. Lucy unpacked the plates and cutlery and
Andy uncorked more wine, splashed it into paper
cups.

'You must come over to us soon,' Lucy invited.
'We have a lovely cottage on the edge of the forest.
The dogs love it and of course they were company
for me when Andy was away...' She went on about
her home and Fenella listened and glanced across
at Sam who sat on a cushion the other side of the
fireplace, absently feeding the dogs titbits of cold
chicken. He looked up and smiled again and then
she understood.

She felt it too, the need to be alone. Andy and
Lucy were good company, were Sam's family,
but...

Fenella's appetite had gone. Another hunger
raged through her. She picked at her chicken, sipped
at her wine, avoiding Sam's eyes upon her. She
sensed him watching her, tried to join in the conversation between husband and wife, failed and
sank into silence, eyes fixed glassily on the wild
flames that leapt in the chimney.

It was getting hotter. The dogs slumped against
her crossed legs, were heavy and hot. Her fingers
moved to loosen the top button of her lacy white

blouse and she caught Sam's eye. He was trans-
fixed, eyes burning with the same need that
throbbed deep inside her. Her fingers froze at first,
terrified that Andy and Lucy would pick up on the
frissons of sensuality that were flying between them,
but then her fingers relaxed.

Slowly she undid the top button and the next,
held Sam's eyes with her own, which were heavy
and sultry as that hot August day. The tips of her
fingers slid under the lacy cotton above her breasts.
Soft movements that were for Sam's eyes only. Her
fingers lingered on her warm flesh, smoothing and
caressing in tiny circles. Sam closed his eyes painfully for a second, opened them and looked away
from her, his fists balled, knuckles white.

The dogs shifted their weight and Fenella drew
her legs up, clutched them tightly and rested her
chin on her knees, her hair falling silkily around
her face, shielding from everyone but Sam the secret
smile and the wordless challenge she threw him. His
eyes held hers in disbelief then he smiled wickedly
as Lucy handed him a plate of gateau. He held his
fork loosely, twirled it very slowly before sinking
it into...

Fenella buried her face in her knees, her shoulders
shaking, trying to control her laughter. When she
looked up, Sam was holding the fork motionless in
front of him, a black cherry pierced on the tip.

Her explosion of laughter fortunately coincided
with the punchline of one of Andy's jokes.

It was difficult to stop Andy once he started and
on any other occasion Fenella would have found

him hysterical, but every time she glanced at Sam she knew what he was thinking.

It was the dogs who were the first to move restlessly and Lucy jumped to her feet. 'We ought to be getting back. The dogs like a run in the forest before their dinner. Let me help you with this stuff, Fenella.'

'Don't worry, Sam and I will clear up after you've gone.'

At the door Lucy turned to Fenella. 'Do come over and see us soon. Now that Sam has got everything sorted out Andy won't be going away again. We can start to enjoy a proper married life together.'

'What did Lucy mean, now that you've got everything sorted out?' Fenella asked after they'd waved them off.

Sam swung her gently back against the door after he'd closed it, held her hands lightly at her sides.

'We will be partners in the new corporation I'm setting up. Now, much as I care for my brother, I could have done without the last hour of his company.'

Fenella laughed. 'Well, you invited them.'

'Yes, short-sighted of me, wasn't it?' He leaned forward and kissed her, lightly at first then deepening to quicken Fenella's heartbeat. When he released her he took her hand and led her to the rugs and cushions in front of the fire. 'Come on, I want to make love to you,' he whispered.

'Sam!' she protested, her mouth curving into a half-smile. She remained standing as Sam sank on to a pile of cushions and poured a paper cup of wine. Suddenly she was nervous, her fears bunching inside her.

He looked up at her, his eyes dark and impenetrable, and held the cup to her. 'Is this what you need?'

She shook her head miserably; it was the last thing she needed, false courage.

'Why won't you lie with me then?' He put the cup down on the hearth and extended his hand to her. Shakily she took it and gently he urged her down. She knelt beside him and he eased a couple of cushions under his head so he could study her. 'Don't you want us to make love?'

'Yes! I mean . . . yes, I do but . . .' She raised her eyes to stare bleakly at the ceiling.

He said softly. 'I love you, Fenella.'

She looked at him then, eyes dimmed with pain. 'You didn't have to say that,' she whispered. 'It was unnecessary.'

'I thought it was what you wanted to hear.'

'Is that why you said it? So that it would make things easier?' she husked bitterly.

He smoothed the back of his hand down the lacy sleeve of her blouse. 'I said it because I meant it, because I wanted you to know that I care deeply for you. I love you and want to make love to you. What do *you* want?'

She closed her eyes for an instance. 'I . . . I don't want sex, not just sex . . .'

'It won't be like that, how can it be?'

'But, Sam . . . a week. We've known each other only a——'

'Seven years and a week,' he grated. 'I want to marry you, Fenella. I've always wanted you.'

She smiled wryly. 'You didn't have to say that either.'

'Can't I say anything right for you?' He smiled.

She couldn't look at him, didn't want to admit all the doubts and fears that tore through her.

'You rejected me once,' she murmured.

'Are you afraid I'll reject you again?' He sat up and reached for her, held her in his arms. 'We are two different people now, Fenella. Then wasn't right, now is.'

'I...I know...but...' She eased him away from her so she could look into his eyes. 'There's been no one, Sam, in those seven years, no one. I couldn't ... just couldn't ...'

'Because of my rejection?' His tone was appalled, his eyes smoked with shock.

She sighed raggedly. 'You see, you're shocked. That was what I was afraid of, that because I'm still ... haven't been with anyone ...'

'That I would think there was something wrong with you? Oh, my darling! I'm only shocked to think of what I did to you that day. I thought——'

'You thought that I was free with my love?' She shook her head. 'Only in my imagination, in my fantasies, and it was always with you.' Her eyes held his. She took a deep breath. 'I have to tell you this, because...because I love you and once you thought me a tramp and I never want you to think that again. I have to tell you this before we let it go any further.'

'Fenella, you don't have to tell me anything.'

'I do, I want to. Since you came back you've made a few remarks and you thought Simon and I were lovers.'

'It doesn't matter any more——'

'It matters to me,' she insisted, her eyes wide and imploring. She took a gulp of breath, wanted it to be over quickly. 'We saw you that day you arrived in your old Mini. Simon laughed. You intrigued me. I wanted to see you again. We passed in the corridor, outside the kitchen. You had a glass of water in your hand——'

'And I was angry,' he interrupted, remembering. 'The meeting wasn't going my way. You were wearing tennis gear.'

Fenella smiled, went on more calmly. 'I think I fell in love with you at that very moment, as you brushed past me. I was thinking of you when... when I was lying on the grass with Simon. Something had changed that day... between me and Simon. Suddenly we weren't kids any more. When he kissed me... when he touched me... it wasn't him... it was you, because that's the way I wanted it to be. I wanted *you* to be making love to me, not Simon. Then you caught us and it made me feel so guilty. I was angry and confused and then I said all those silly things to you and then, because you were there, I wanted you more than ever.'

'And I turned you away.' Sam shook his head. 'I didn't know, Fenella. How could I?'

'I felt cheap and dirty. I'd nearly let Simon make love to me because I was fantasising about you. It made me feel there was something wrong with me, made me feel so guilty. I spent seven years dreaming about you, wanting you.'

'We all have our dreams and hopes and sometimes the only way to realise them is in our minds.'

Fenella's eyes were wide. 'Do you do that, dream and fantasise?'

Sam smiled and brushed her hair from her face. 'Oh, yes. I haven't been able to get a certain beautiful child-woman out of my mind for those same seven years. So you see, I too had my dreams, but dreams are for living, darling.'

He leaned forward and touched her lips with his, a teasing, tantalising gesture that uncoiled the doubts and fears inside her. She clung to him, inhaling his warm scent deeply, wanting him to be melded to her heart forever.

Sam drew her down beside him, sprawled on the rugs and cushions. He held her in his arms, wrapped his warmth and love around her till she felt safe and right as if it had always been meant to be.

When she was relaxed and suppliant against him his mouth closed over hers, his tongue seeking more, urging hers to venture to him. She knew so little, she thought, in that moment of ecstatic exploration. He would be disappointed with her, frustrated by her naïveté and inexperience.

He sensed her hesitation, drew his mouth from hers, whispered against her cheeks. 'It's all right. Don't be afraid. Let me look at you, Fenella.' He lay back against the cushions, on his side, supported on one elbow. He gazed down at her, moved her hand to the buttons of her blouse. 'Don't ever be shy with me, darling. You're too lovely to hide anything from me. We belong together and nothing matters but us.' He smiled down at her. 'For all your innocence you knew what you were doing when you started to undo your buttons.'

'Did I drive you crazy?' she murmured with a smile.

'You know you did, but you can't leave a job half done.'

She lowered her dark lashes in a moment of shyness, knowing what he wanted her to do.

She watched the hunger in his eyes as softly, slowly she undid the next tiny glass button and then the next. She was shocked at the pleasure she felt at the tension rising in him, the tiny muscle at his jaw strained. All the buttons were free now and gently she eased the white lace from the tight waistband of her jeans.

He made no attempt to touch her but his eyes drank in every sensuous movement she made. She wore no bra and the lace gaped slightly, exposing only a promise.

'Touch yourself, Fenella,' he urged softly. 'I want to see you touch your breasts.'

With a small smile she obeyed, for him and for herself. She let her fingers graze over her own heated flesh, gingerly at first and then, seeing the arousal in his dark features, his breath quickening, she became less inhibited, more daring. Her breasts swelled in her own caress, her dark nipples peaked in despair. It wasn't enough. Slowly, tremulously she lowered herself to him. He was waiting, his mouth hard and hot. As he took her nipple between his lips they both uttered a moan of sweet pleasure and desire.

Fenella collapsed across him, and with a smooth, swift movement he rolled them both over till he had her beneath him.

He held back from her, looking down into her face. 'You are so beautiful, the most perfect creature,' he murmured deep in his throat. His lips came to hers and she parted hers swiftly, impatiently. Pain and desire scorched through her, leaving wheals of white heat that ached and pulsed through her body.

Sam peeled her jeans from her hips and thighs and she shuddered against him, feeling the coarseness of his jeans on her searing flesh. Desperately she struggled with the belt at his waist, moaned in frustration when it didn't give. He laughed softly, helped her, laughed softly again when she gasped in wonderment.

Fine white lace of her skimpy briefs was all that was left between them. Sam slid his fingers between the soft cotton and her flaming flesh. Fenella moaned and bit her lip as he stroked and caressed the soft triangle of jet hair. His hands moved to her bottom, eased the fabric from her smooth skin, drew her hard against him.

His exploration of her body was sweet torture. Her flesh blazed with a need she was fighting to hold in check. She wanted him inside her, to appease the pain and the hunger, and yet she wanted the exquisite sensations he aroused in her, with his mouth and hands, to last forever.

There was no shyness with him now; they were as one in their love and need to please. Fenella gave in return every divine pleasure he gifted her with. Her lips, mouth and tongue sought and caressed and crazed with a fire that had him crying out in an anguish of delight. Fire and heat, pain and pleasure powered through their strained bodies.

His mouth on hers stifled the cry of pain and joy as at last he thrust into her, strong yet holding back for fear of hurting her more. She ground against him, the need for satisfaction more urgent than anything in her life before. He was like taut silk inside her, moving, thrusting, pulsing till she shuddered against him, liquid gold vaporising deep inside her. The heated sensation throbbed through her, not stilling or quenching the hunger but surging it forward, again and again. The rush of energy inside her powered him on—almost violently he moved against her, pumping small moans of erotic abandonment from her lips and then, with a deep spasm that had them both crying out with the miracle of vibrating ecstasy, he shuddered helplessly, trembling against her sated body.

They lay together, wrapped in each other's embrace, exhausted yet euphoric. There were no words to be spoken. Fenella knew a fulfilment and a completeness far outreaching anything her fantasies had conjured up in those lost years without him. Sam Ballantine was her life.

CHAPTER EIGHT

THEIR work kept them apart more than they wished. Several times over the next two weeks Sam had to travel up north to his factory. Too few nights they spent at home at Hunstand Manor, and when they did there were numerous interruptions. The phone seemed to ring incessantly for Sam. And last weekend Mercedes had descended on them and she and Sam had spent hours incarcerated in the study. She'd stayed the whole weekend and only Simon's intervention had saved Fenella and Sam from rowing. He was besotted with Sam's secretary and had whisked her off to a night-club on Saturday night, leaving Sam and Fenella to snatch a few precious hours together.

'Is this how it's always going to be?' Fenella asked wearily, flopping into the armchair by the fire in the study. She'd been late again tonight, not by choice—a late client without an appointment had held her up. It was one of the nights when Sam had been working at home all day and had expected her to be back in time to join him for dinner. He'd eaten alone.

Sam poured her a brandy. 'You could give up work, you know. Once we are married there will be more than enough to do at the Grange.'

149

'You're beginning to sound like my father.' She grinned ruefully.

'He has some points. After all, you don't *have* to work.'

Fenella watched him moving restlessly around the study. The last few days he'd seemed distracted, not quite his exuberant self. He was overworking and the strain was beginning to show.

'If and when I give up my company, it will by my choice, not anyone else's,' she told him firmly.

'Am I included in that sweeping "anyone else's"?' he grated back at her, pausing in front of a framed photograph of a Trent family gathering.

Fenella got up and went to him, linked her arm in his and leaned her head on his shoulder. 'I'm sorry, darling. We're both tired. Let's not talk business.' He kissed the top of her head. She smiled. 'That's better. That's an old picture of my family,' she told him, wanting to change the subject. Pointing to a grey-haired gentleman seated at the same mahogany desk they were standing by, she murmured, 'My grandfather. He died before I was born . . .'

Sam stiffened next to her and Fenella bit her lip. How insensitive of her. He had no family portraits, no one left from his past. And now, because he was so obviously tired, wasn't the time to ask him about his parents and their tragic deaths.

'I'll make some more coffee before we go up,' she suggested, moving away from him to the door.

'None for me, Fenella. I want to sleep tonight. Your father will be home tomorrow and we have a lot of work to get through.'

'Sam?' Fenella frowned, stepping towards him. 'They aren't due back till the weekend.'

He looked at her guiltily, ran a hand through his hair. 'He called today, something's cropped up and they'll be here tomorrow. I'm sorry, I forgot to tell you when you came in.'

'Forgot! Sam, how could you?' she cried.

'Look, I've apologised; what more do you want, blood?' He snapped irritably and then as quickly as his temper had risen it was gone. He took her swiftly in his arms, held her close. 'Darling, forgive me.'

'Oh, Sam,' she moaned, sliding her arms comfortingly around him. 'You're exhausted, you know?'

'And so are you.' He looked down into her drawn features and smiled. 'What we need is an early night.' She knew what he meant.

Their lovemaking that night was different, more urgent than usual. After, they lay in each other's arms, but Sam wasn't at ease. He murmured that he was going back to his room, kissed her softly and left her. Fenella reasoned that he was probably restless because her father was due home the next day and this would be the last time they could make love so freely. It wouldn't be right for him to come to her room every night as he had done. Not that they had been completely at ease before. Neither had wanted to be seen openly living together in front of the staff and they had been very discreet, Sam leaving her in the early hours to sleep in his own bed. It had been a strain.

'I won't go into the office today,' Fenella told Sam at breakfast the next morning. 'My father and Adrianna will expect me to be here when they get back.'

'I thought you said you had a lot of work on.'

'I have, but——'

'I'll be here all day; besides, I expect they'll be pretty tired when they get in.'

Fenella glanced at her watch. 'Yes, I suppose you're right.' She got up from the breakfast bar. 'I'll try and get home early.' She hesitated. 'Sam, will you tell my father, about us?' She had wanted to tell him on the few occasions he had rung from the Seychelles but Sam had said it would be better to wait till he got home. Fenella had not seen what difference it would make but hadn't argued.

'No. I'll wait till you are home and we can tell him together.' He smiled at her and she bent and kissed him goodbye.

Odd, but she felt restless on the train. It was a glorious, golden autumn day, misty and bronzed, and she should have been ecstatically happy, but something niggled deep inside her. She loved Sam, he loved her, she had no doubts about that, but since that wonderful afternoon at the Grange when they had sealed their love Sam had sometimes seemed distanced from her. She'd not made anything of it, knowing pressure of work was more than likely the reason.

Her day was a heavy one. Shivers on the Stock Exchange were panicking a lot of clients and nerves needed soothing. Then Italy devalued the lira and there was minor chaos for several hours. Fenella was red-eyed from the computer and exhausted by late afternoon.

She left the city in the middle of the rush-hour and by the time she unlocked her car in the station car park she had a blinding headache to go with it. She drove home quickly, eager to see her father and Adrianna, eager to be with Sam to tell everyone their news.

Joseph Trent's Rolls-Royce was parked outside the Manor, so Fenella knew they were home. Joan was in the hall waiting for her when she burst into the front door; there was no beaming smile on her face as Fenella would have expected at the return of her employer.

'Adrianna is upstairs resting,' she quickly told Fenella. 'Your father and Mr Ballantine——'

'What's wrong?'

Joan wrung her hands in anguish. 'Your father . . . he started on poor Mr Ballantine as soon as he set foot in the house. Said some terrible things. Oh, Fenella, I shouldn't gossip like this but I didn't want you bursting in on them——'

'Where are they?' Fenella asked weakly, her eyes dark with misery. Whatever had Sam done to deserve this?

'In the study, but don't go in. They are raging at each other. Fenella! Don't!'

Ignoring her, Fenella shot away, her high heels clicking impatiently on the parquet. Joan gave a small moan of anguish and started up the stairs to the bedrooms.

Fenella stopped dead outside the study door, tugged at her suit jacket in an effort to compose herself. Anger with her father burned inside her... She heard voices, harsh, bitter, angry words that stilled her heart till it almost stopped beating.

'I'll take you to court if I have to... you have no right... a partnership, I said, not this!' Her father's furious voice froze Fenella's hand on the door-knob.

'I'm sorry I dragged you back from your honeymoon but I'm saving you from yourself if you did but know it. You have no choice, Joe, no choice whatsoever. If you want to play dirty with me, go ahead. It'll get you nowhere, only do harm to yourself and Fenella——'

'Keep my daughter out of this!'

'I wish that I could! A minor point while we are on the subject.' Sam's voice was biting. 'Why didn't you level with her before I arrived? What the hell did you hope to gain by keeping this from her?'

'And what the blazes is it to you?' There was a pause and then Joseph Trent's voice lowered threateningly. 'Have you been messing with her?'

'We're going to be married.'

In the deathly silence that followed Fenella struggled to find the strength to open the door and walk in but in vain. Faint with shock, she leaned her throbbing head against the door-jamb and then the words that followed shattered her so completely she thought her heart would stop.

'You bastard!' Her father's voice rattled in his throat with fury. Slowly and deliberately he went on, 'When I said the only way to get your thieving hands on my companies was to marry my daughter I never thought you'd take up the challenge. Now, get out of my house before I shotgun you out!'

Fenella moved then, blindly, weakly she staggered to the kitchen. It was the nearest refuge. She stood by the window, shaking from head to toe, tears of bitterness unshed and burning the backs of her eyes. Her hands clung to the stainless steel sink for support, then nausea cramped her stomach and she retched.

It was Joan's safe, comforting hands that prised hers from the sink. Fenella flung herself in her arms and cried like a child.

Joan said nothing, stroked her hair as she used to when Nanny Parkins's discipline had driven Fenella tempestuously to the flat above the garages.

'Don't cry now, Fenella. Hush.'

With one last sob of anguish, Fenella straightened herself up. She wasn't a child any more. She was a grown woman, running a successful company. She raked her fingers through her jet hair, raised a weak smile for Joan. 'I'm all right now, Joan, thank you. Would...would you make me some tea...and bring it up to my room...and...and a couple of aspirins? Not yet, though... In about fifteen minutes.'

That was all it should take, probably less. What could you say to a bastard like that?

Instinct powered her upstairs to his bedroom. He would be packing, nervously no doubt, fearful that her father would carry out his threat and shoot him.

She knocked and walked straight in without waiting for an answer. Sam Ballantine was showing no fear or hurry to leave. He was on the phone, half perched on the dressing-table by the window. In black cords and grey Viyella shirt he looked casually at ease.

'You can reach me via the car phone. I'll be at the Grange from now on... No, Mercedes...that's not necessary...the weekend will be fine ... I'll be back by then. The meetings with the directors of Trent's shouldn't take more than a day... Yes, and you.' He got the receiver down, turned to her with a smile.

Her eyes blazed. 'Arranging a cosy weekend with your secretary?'

His smile faded. 'Fenella...' He stepped towards her.

Fenella instinctively stepped back, the back of her heel clicking on the door. 'Don't come near me!' she warned with a hiss. 'I was outside the study door, heard enough to hate you from the bottom of my soul!'

His eyes darkened momentarily. 'And what exactly did you hear?'

'That you want to marry me so you can get a slice of Trent Industries.'

A very dark brow rose. He studied her angry features before saying quietly and coolly, 'Are you sure you heard right?'

Clenching her fists tightly at her side, she breathed flintily. 'Not exactly those very words but something not far short of it.'

He held her gaze for a second before moving across the room to his black pigskin suitcases. He threw them on the bed, clicked them open. 'I can see by your face and hear by your tone that it is useless to argue with you.'

'Why should you argue with me when it's true?' she retorted sharply. 'You're nothing but a cheap opportunist!'

He looked up at her from the chest of drawers he was gathering his clothes from, his mouth thinning angrily. 'Look up your family tree to find a cheap opportunist, sweetheart. And I don't have to marry you for a slice of Trent Industries; it's already mine!' He flung an armful of clothes into the suitcase and crossed to the wardrobe.

Stunned, Fenella gaped at him, struggling for breath. 'What . . . what do you mean?'

'Ask your father!' he retorted without looking at her.

'No! I damn well won't!' she cried, crossing the room and grabbing hold of his arm angrily. 'I want to hear it from you!'

Fiercely he wrenched her hand from him. Gripping her upper arms, he almost shook her. 'Well, you won't! You'll get the whole sordid story from him and no one else. I've done what I had to do. I've done it cleanly and efficiently. My brother and I now own Trent Industries and if you want a post-mortem on it ask your father to do the honours!'

He let her go, so suddenly that she staggered. 'I knew it,' she breathed heavily. 'I knew the minute you stepped into this house that you were up to no good. My father had good reason to throw you out seven years ago, didn't he? What was it...blackmail?'

'Don't be so bloody melodramatic, Fenella.' He slammed a case shut, started on another.

'You're the one striving for an Oscar! All this mystery and suspense. If you won't tell me what's going on, I'll tell you, shall I?' He didn't answer, infuriating her even more by going on with his packing as if she were nothing but an irritating fly buzzing round his head. 'Somehow, I don't know how, probably with the same charisma you charmed Joan and the rest of the staff with, you persuaded my father to let you live here while he was on his honeymoon. You've rifled through his safe, found out all you could about his companies...then you...then you...'

'Then what, Fenella?' He stood with his hands on his hips, waiting for her to go on.

'Somehow...somehow...you've taken over. Snatched my father's companies... and...'

'And what?' he echoed darkly.

Suddenly her eyes filled. Swallowing the lump in her throat she battled on, her head spinning with doubts. 'Then to secure yourself even more...you...you made me love you.' Suddenly that was even worse than any harm he'd done to her father. She'd loved him, completely, utterly, hopelessly. He'd betrayed her so deeply, so efficiently that she would carry the scars in her heart forever.

'You never loved me, did you?' Her voice was little above a hoarse whisper. 'You used me, seduced me with your smile...don't come near me!' She held both hands up defensively. If he touched her it would be the end.

Sam stopped in the middle of the room, ran a hand feverishly over his forehead. 'Please don't, Fenella,' he grated raggedly. 'I can't bear it. Don't think that of me.'

'I don't think, I know. I understand it all now. You've never meant a word of love you've whispered to me. I...I saved myself for you. Seven years of my life...' Her voice broke on a sob of despair. 'You stripped me of everything. I told you things...everything I ever felt for you. You cheated me.'

'I love you, Fenella, believe me. I've always loved you. You've been my spur all these years...'

'Yes, so that you could come back and rob my father of his life!' she bit back, some inner strength rallying her. 'I'll tell you one more thing before you leave this house forever. You were my spur too. When you insulted me that day by the river-bank, it changed my life. You made me see myself for the first time. I didn't like the rich spoilt bitch I was turning into. Because of you I worked and studied and missed out on growing up because deep inside me I wanted to prove that I wasn't a bird-brain. I can't explain...just a feeling I had that one day you might come back. I wanted to be somebody for you,' she ended on a whisper. Bravely, she drew herself up, proudly tilted her chin. 'Thank God I did, because it's all I've got left now. Once, you were my fantasy. Now I know you to be nothing but a figment of my adolescent imagination. I hate you, Sam Ballantine...'

'Don't, Fenella...' he implored.

'I hate you only marginally more than myself.' With a cynical laugh she looked at him for the last time. 'You're getting thrown out of this house yet again; there won't be a third time because if you ever come near me, my father or Hunstand Manor again, I'll take a gun to you myself!'

She slammed out of his bedroom into her own, kicked off her shoes and stood by the window, shaking with rage and humiliation. Her mind refused to function, buzzed with a red mist that refused to shift. She held her head in her hands, willing the pain to go.

There was a light tap on her door and she called out, incoherently. 'Leave...me alone...I...don't... Keep away from me!'

The door opened and Joan came in with a tray of tea. Fenella collapsed into a heap on the bed. In silence Joan poured her a cup of tea, her hand hovering over the sugar bowl at the slamming of Sam's bedroom door. There was no other sound till the thud of the front door and then seconds later the thud of a car door, an engine revving de-

terminedly, gravel spurting and then a soft drone
fading into the distance.

The silence that followed was deathly. With a
moan Fenella sat up, nervously flicked her hair
from her tear-stained face, looked bleakly into
Joan's kindly eyes.

'Tea and sympathy,' Joan said softly and sat
down next to her on the bed.

Fenella drank her tea thirstily, swallowed two
aspirins and told Joan everything. Her love for
Sam, his apparent love for her, her hopes and
dreams.

'He betrayed me, Joan. He and my father.'

Joan held her hand soothingly. 'You don't know
that, Fenella. You heard snatches of conversation
that could be interpreted in so many different ways.'

Fenella shook her head dismally. 'My father
wouldn't have thrown him out if it wasn't true. I
know I don't know the full story yet, but I know
enough. Sam wouldn't tell me it all, insisted it must
come from my father, but what difference will it
make? Sam wanted to marry me for Trent
Industries, not for myself, and if that weren't
enough apparently he has control of everything my
father and his forefathers worked so hard for.'

With a deep sigh, not understanding, Joan said,
'I can't believe that Mr Ballantine would do something underhand, Fenella. He's such a lovely
man——'

'Oh, yes. That was part of his wicked scheme,'
Fenella interrupted bitterly. 'We were all fooled,
weren't we?'

'I've always been a pretty good judge of character, Dennis too, and your father, he wouldn't have been fooled by him,' Joan reasoned.

'Great! And me? I must be the prize idiot of the year!'

Joan laughed softly. 'I didn't mean that, but that should prove my point. None of us is fools, Fenella. Look, why don't you talk to your father? He owes it to you to give you a full explanation.'

'Maybe I don't want to hear any more,' she said, tight-lipped.

'Now that is talking silly.' Joan got up. 'I'll run you a nice hot bath to soothe away that headache of yours. When you feel better, go down and talk with your father. By then you both will have calmed down.'

Fenella looked up at her. 'Where's Adrianna?'

'Still resting. She was upset by the row, took to her bed. She's not strong like you, Fenella. All she wants is a quiet life with your father.'

'Thanks to Sam Ballantine, she'll get just that,' Fenella stated ruefully. Her eyes widened painfully. 'What is my father going to do now, Joan? His work was his life.'

Shaking her head Joan answered wearily, 'I don't know. That's something only he can answer.' She went through to the bathroom.

Later, when Fenella was soaking the ache from her limbs in the bath, she heard Joan moving round in the next room, stripping Sam's bed, tidying the room. It was all so final.

Joseph Trent was still at his desk in the study when Fenella went downstairs. Her headache had lifted but her heart lay as heavy as a stone inside her. The sight of her father's haggard features under his deep tan tugged it to life. She went to him and with a sob hugged him tightly.

'Oh, Dad, I'm so sorry. I heard, when you were arguing with Sam. I blame myself. I shouldn't have——'

'Come on now, pet. Don't upset yourself.' He held her fiercely. 'I can take all this. I don't want you going to pieces.'

She looked up at him and gave him a tearful smile. 'I'm not going to pieces. I'm not a Trent for nothing, you know.'

'A Trent,' he murmured regretfully. 'Once that name meant something——'

'And it will again,' Fenella insisted. 'Dad, I don't know all the details but you're not going to let him get away with this are you? He's a cheat, a fraud and——'

'Don't, Fenella.' He drew away from her, slumped down into his chair and stared pitifully at the mass of papers strewn across his desk-top. 'There's nothing I can do.'

Fenella steeled herself, lifted her chin. 'We're family, Dad. Whatever Sam Ballantine has done, we'll fight him.'

He smiled grimly. 'Sam Ballantine *is* family, Fenella.'

Swaying slightly, she gripped the edge of the desk. After a long agonised second she husked incredulously, 'What do you mean?'

He gazed at her, eyes deep set and pained. 'Sit down, love.'

Fenella collapsed on to a chair, her head swimming.

'Sam is my first cousin once removed. I don't know what you heard or what Sam has told you——'

'He's told me nothing!' Fenella blurted. 'Nothing!'

'His father, John Ballantine, was my cousin. Your grandfather, George Trent, married Emma Ballantine, sister of Silas Ballantine, John's father, so your grandfather was John's uncle by marriage, Sam's great-uncle.'

Fenella's eyes shot to the photograph on the wall, remembering Sam stiffening at the sight of him, stiffening as if he hated him.

In a whisper Fenella asked, 'What has that to do with now?'

'According to Sam, Trent Industries is his.'

'How can that be?' Fenella exploded. 'Just because he's some relative doesn't give him a claim on us. He's a Ballantine, not a Trent. What do you mean, "according to Sam"? Is he lying?'

Joseph Trent drew his brows together with his fingers. Fenella hated Sam even more for the stress he was putting her father through.

'At first I thought he was, but he's clever, I'll give him that. He produced overwhelming evidence to prove we are related.'

'But how come you didn't know before? I mean, you must have known you had a cousin John and two cousins once removed, Sam and his brother Andrew.'

'The families weren't close. Emma's brother, Silas Ballantine, lived in Canada. There was no contact between the two families, not until his son John Ballantine came back to his roots.'

'He died,' Fenella murmured. 'Sam told me his father had died in an accident and six months later his mother committed suicide. The boys were brought up in orphanages.'

'So he's had a tough life,' her father stated, getting up from the desk and pacing the room. The near brutality of his tone had Fenella looking at him sharply as he ranted on. 'That doesn't give him cause to make mine a nightmare. Damn him! Damn him to hell!'

'He . . . he must have reason to believe he has a claim.'

Her father didn't seem to hear her, pacing the room furiously. 'The young upstart! How dare he do this, pussy-foot his way into my home? Lay claim to my life's work and have the nerve to mess with my daughter!'

Fenella's heart beat unsteadily. She stood up and looked at her father uncertainly. What would he think of her for giving herself to such a man?

Joseph Trent turned to her, his eyes narrowed menacingly. 'Keep away from him!' His index finger came up warningly. 'I don't know what's been going on under my roof while I was away and I don't want to know—spare me the sordid details— but don't ever see him again, do you hear? He's on the make that one, just like his father before him. If you have any love and respect for your own father you'll forget his existence. Don't mention the name of Sam Ballantine in this house again. Have I made myself clear?'

Wide-eyed, Fenella stared back at him. 'Yes, Father,' she murmured, and turned and walked shakily from the room.

Upstairs in her room, she sat by the window, staring bleakly out into darkness, clutching herself for comfort. She was twenty-three and her father had just wiped away ten years of that. She felt like a child again, being reprimanded for some mis-demeanour and sent to bed. But hadn't her father always treated her like a child? Denying her any involvement with Trent Industries was tantamount to saying she wasn't old enough and mature enough.

But that wasn't the cause of the deep hurt inside her now. The worst thing of all was the feeling of shame that swamped her. Spare me the sordid details, her father had stated. She had never seen her love-affair with Sam as sordid, on reflection foolish maybe, but never sordid. But her father had seen it that way, just as Sam had seen it that way when he had come across her and Simon on the

river-bank. Shuddering at the thought, she suppressed a moan of anguish.

Much later, she lay in bed, exhausted but unable
to sleep. Joan had tried to coax her downstairs to
eat with her father but she had refused. Even
refused to go and talk to Adrianna, who had roused
herself and was asking to see her. Tomorrow, she
had promised, and with a sigh Joan had left her to
her misery.

There was still so much she didn't know and
understand. She doubted if she would learn any
more from her father. His last words had been so
bitterly dismissive. Sam was the only one with the
answers now.

I still love him, was the conclusion she came to
in the early hours of the morning. Even hate and
anger and bitterness couldn't quash that. She had
never known such happiness as these last weeks,
and the misery to come would be the worst of her
life. A life without him was inconceivable but inevitable. She had to draw strength from some inner
source and go on with her life. She'd leave her
father's home of course. It was time. Hunstand
Manor held bitter memories now.

Drowsiness finally overcame her as the grandfather clock in the hall echoed three desolate
chimes. Sam would be sleeping now, on some
makeshift bed upstairs in the sunset room of Lytton
Grange. The room she would have been sharing
with him in the future if he hadn't betrayed her
love. Had he ever loved her? she questioned
miserably. He couldn't have done; if he had he

wouldn't have bowed to her father's threats. He would have taken her with him, explained away her doubts and fears, loved her into the long night.

Instead, she was alone, as alone as a drifting, oarless boat on a sea of turmoil.

CHAPTER NINE

'CAN you believe that?' Fenella stormed, throwing her car keys down on the breakfast bar. '*She* was there! He couldn't wait, could he?'

Joan plugged in the kettle and smiled, the sudden rush of warmth to her face belying the strain she had been under this past week. 'Well, your anger is a step up from your depression. Shows there is life where we all thought there wasn't. Who was there?'

'The secretary, Miss Mercedes Benz herself!'

'Her surname isn't Benz, is it?'

'Oh, Joan,' Fenella reluctantly smiled, 'what would I do without you?'

'Wither away to nothing, no doubt.' She took a plate of lasagne from the microwave and pushed it in front of Fenella. 'Now eat before you fade away like the ghost that haunts this house. One of you is enough.'

Fenella perched on a bar stool and picked at the food with uninterest. 'Is there really a ghost here, some tormented soul ghouling away? I've never seen it.'

Joan made tea. 'Nor has anyone else, but houses like this wouldn't be the same without the thought of one. Now don't think you're fooling me with

169

this sudden interest in ghosts. Tell me what happened.'

Fenella shrugged dismissively. 'Nothing. When I got there her car was parked outside in the driveway. I reversed out. I won't go back again, Joan. You know how much courage it took to go chasing after him in the first place.' She shook her head decisively. 'I won't go again.'

'You're using his secretary as an excuse, Fenella. You know full well there is nothing going on between them. She's his secretary, an attractive one, and that's all.'

'I know,' Fenella conceded. 'But she was there nevertheless. I couldn't have gone in...' The phone rang. 'I'll take it, Joan; it's probably Adrianna checking to see if I'm still in the land of the living. She's taken all this so badly.'

'Haven't we all?' Joan chipped bleakly as Fenella picked up the wall phone.

'Hello.'

'You never were much good at reversing.'

The blood drained from her face at the sound of his voice.

'What do you want?' she asked coolly, frowning at Joan as her face lit up.

'I could ask you the same question. You were hardly out for a drive and took a wrong turning.'

'You saw me?'

'Heard you. Couldn't fail to recognise your grating reverse gear. Remind me to give you some driving lessons some time.' There was humour in his voice, which only served to feed Fenella's anger. 'Mercedes has gone now. I want you to come back.'

'My father wouldn't like it——'

'Your father can go to hell.'

'There's no need to be abusive——'

'After what I've taken from him these last three days that's baby talk.'

'You've seen him?'

'I've been with him at the works in Northumbria. Can't say we've parted the best of friends but there's hope for him yet. I'll see you when you get here.' The line went dead.

Fenella held the receiver in numb fingers before Joan prised it away from her.

'Mr Ballantine?'

'The devil himself. He wants me to go over.'

Joan beamed from ear to ear. 'Well, go on, then.'

It wasn't that easy. It had taken a week of confidence-stroking before Joan had persuaded her to go to Sam. Seeing Mercedes's car parked outside had wiped out that confidence. But she *had* to see him, for no other reason than to satisfy herself that it was all over, though she knew with depressing certainty that it was.

So why was she hurtling dangerously through narrow country lanes to go to him? Because of her obstinate father, that was why. He'd flown up north, with a dutiful wife complacently in tow, after refusing to waste any more breath on the subject of the infamous Sam Ballantine. And there was another reason too, one which had hit her midriff with the impact of a heavyweight's punch. She was a Trent, Joseph Trent's sole issue, as lawyers referred to beneficiaries, and she had rights. She was her father's daughter and if—God forbid—anything happened to him, she was his heir. So if Sam Ballantine was cheating her father out of his companies he was cheating her too. Snatching from under her feet what was rightfully hers.

She couldn't get out of the car when she arrived. Just sat staring out of the windscreen at the Grange with its strange turrets and heavily leaded windows catching the autumn sun. She might have shared all this with Sam... Her nerve nearly broke when he stepped out of the front door to come to her.

He looked different. His zest for life had been drained from him. His jeans were paint-spattered, his Arran sweater hung baggily from his wide shoulders, his black hair was dishevelled, his tan sadly depleted now. A week of undermining her father had done that to him and she wasn't sorry. He deserved more.

She got out of the car and walked towards him, plunging her hands deeply into her jeans pockets so that he wouldn't notice how they shook.

'You look a mess.' Were her first words born out of a confusion of shyness and embarrassment? She shouldn't have come. All her nerve, like a coward facing the enemy, had fled her.

'You don't look so bright yourself.'

She'd made an effort with her appearance, makeup and her hair fluffed wildly around her face, but not to disarm him, to show she was getting on with her life without him. To no avail apparently. If she had recognised his misery, he had hers.

'Thanks for the compliment,' was the only cryptic remark she could force to her tight lips.

They walked to the house. Sam opened the door. A fire blazed in the hall and Fenella's heart jerked, memories flooding her of the first fire in the house. This time was different, though, not because of the new iron fire basket the logs crackled furiously in, but because they were two strangers now, lovers no more.

'Do you want a coffee?' Sam asked brusquely.

'Yes, please.' She didn't follow him to the kitchen but stayed by the fire, sat on a packing case and waited, her nerves stretched to stress point. There were packing cases strewn everywhere. The rest of his belongings had arrived from Saudi. She looked away from them, despising her curiosity. His possessions, his life. The life she had so desperately wanted to share.

'Instant, I'm afraid, and tinned milk. I haven't organised a milkman yet.' He handed her a mug of steaming coffee.

'Where are you sleeping?'

'Upstairs, in our room.'

She smiled at that. So like him.

'I'll never share that room with you,' she told him bleakly.

He sat across from her, on a packing case stamped 'Dubai'.

'You will. I don't expect my wife to sleep anywhere else but in my bed.'

She smiled again, not amused, just amazed at him. She shook her head. 'We'll never marry, not now.'

He cupped his hands around his mug of coffee. 'We will, if I have to throw you over my shoulder and carry you down the aisle with your knickers showing...'

'Sam!' Her eyes shone painfully. 'Don't joke like that!'

'I thought it would make you laugh.'

'At a time like this, nothing is funny,' she iced back angrily. 'I didn't come here for your irreverent witticisms——'

'What did you come for, then?' he asked wearily. 'More abuse?'

'Why bother? You know what a bastard you are without my repeating myself.' Her strength was coming back. 'I came to find out more. Why you think you have the right to crush my father, and me, come to that.'

He eyed her darkly. 'Worried about your inheritance?'

She flushed at that and he smiled cynically. 'Don't worry, I wouldn't cheat you out of what is rightfully yours, that's a Trent trait I wouldn't like to echo. You'll get your dues when the time comes.'

'If it comes from you, I don't want it. I don't want anything the Ballantines have usurped from us!'

'It's obvious your father still hasn't come clean.'

'What do you mean?'

'Would you believe me if I told you?' He raised a jet brow.

Fenella sighed wearily. 'I'm so confused I don't know what to believe. I feel as if I'm being torn apart inside. I love . . . I love my father.'

'And do you love me?'

She couldn't answer, couldn't look at him. She stared into the fire, the flames of hell.

'I know fires are for staring into, but can't you bring yourself to face me and put me out of my misery?'

Bravely she raised violet eyes to his. 'Are you in misery?'

'What do you think? I love you, Fenella. I can't imagine life without you,' he told her emotionally.

'But . . . but you didn't come back. My father ordered you out of the house and you just went. I can't believe you were afraid he would carry out his threat and shoot you.'

His eyes smoked with humour. 'A hero I am not, Fenella. I didn't come this far to risk having my head blown off by an irate industrialist. I've put your father through so much lately that I wouldn't put murder past him.'

'So it's true, you are crushing him.'

'Believe me, Fenella, if it meant losing you I'd pull out of this whole sordid business.'

'How can I believe that when I heard what my father said . . . that he didn't expect you to pick up the challenge when he said the only way you'd get your hands on his companies would be to marry me?'

'Oh, Fenella, sweetheart. It was something snapped out in anger years ago and reiterated again in anger the other day. Do you honestly believe me capable of such a thing? Believe that I could make love to you the way I do without loving you deeply?' He reached for her hand. 'For me, darling, it would be a physical impossibility.'

The warmth of his hand on hers nearly swayed her. Hadn't she wrestled with those very thoughts every miserable night without him? She withdrew her hand from under his. Nevertheless . . .

'You were strange with me before my father returned. I didn't understand before but after . . . after I heard you rowing with my father, I thought that you must have been feeling guilty . . . that it was true, you wanted to marry me for Trent Industries . . .'

'I was feeling guilty,' he admitted honestly, 'not for that reason, though. You told me how much you wanted a seat on your father's board; I knew that wasn't possible. My anger was also building up because he hadn't told you what was going on. He should have done. You had a right to know. I couldn't tell you because it wasn't my place to.'

'Why didn't he tell me, Sam?'

'I can only presume shame, not his but for his father.'

'Shame? I don't understand. I *want* to know the truth. All I know is that you are related to us by marriage and you somehow believe that Trent Industries is rightfully yours and you are putting some sort of squeeze on my father.'

'That's it, is it?'

She nodded her head. 'He was too angry to tell me more.'

'I understand how he feels. I tried the softly, softly approach with him years ago but he just roared like an enraged lion, so I roared back. It took me seven years to put myself into a position to attack. This sort of thing takes money, a lot of money.' He paused. 'Fenella, initially I only intended to take my fair share, what was due to me and Andrew, but the way things have turned out I'm forced to take it all, for your father's sake and yours.'

Fenella steeled herself, sensing she wasn't going to like what was coming. 'I don't understand.'

'I'll start from the beginning.' Sam took a deep breath. 'Your grandfather, George Trent, was a poor manager. He ran the company into debt. The business was floundering——'

'My grandfather was very successful!' Fenella protested, eyes bright with a flare of temper. 'He built the company——'

'He did nothing but fall into debt and nearly finish Trent's empire for good!' Sam told her emphatically.

Fenella shot to her feet. 'That's a lie!'

'Sit down, Fenella,' Sam ordered lightly. 'That was precisely your father's attitude when I told him the truth. Indignation and anger, and I understand, I really do. No one likes to hear ill of their nearest and dearest.'

'And I suppose that is leading up to you telling me my father is no good either! I don't have to listen to this——'

'I thought that was why you came here,' he barked, getting to his feet and snatching at her wrist as she turned to the door. 'For heaven's sake, Fenella, grow up, hear me out. But, I warn you, it gets worse.' His grip tightened as she tried to wriggle free. 'Please, Fenella, if you have any feelings for me, sit down!'

'This isn't an admittance of my feelings,' she snapped as she bumped back down on the packing case. 'Go on, tell me the rest—it can't get much worse. You've already dragged me and my father through the mire; you might as well finish off the rest of the Trent dynasty.'

Ignoring her outburst, he went on. 'My father, John Ballantine, was born and brought up in Canada, made a fortune out of timber but was restless, came back to England to find his roots. He met and married my mother and looked around for new opportunities. Found them in his uncle, George Trent. Your grandfather was making a mess of the business he had taken over from his father. My own father injected money, new ideas into the foundering company. But for all my father's brilliance and flair—and probably because he was dealing with his uncle—he let the legalities slide. Oh, there was an exchange of letters, but no division of shares. I don't think for a minute that your grandfather intended to swindle my father...'

Fenella trapped a cry of anguish in her throat, held her head in her hands. Sam touched her knee lightly.

'I'm sorry, Fenella. It's not pleasant, I know, but very necessary.'

She nodded, lifted her head. 'Go on.'

'My father was killed in an accident, that you know, a car accident, before any proper papers could be drawn up. Your grandfather couldn't resist the temptation to say nothing, carried on with my father's money and ideas as if they were his own.'

'Is that what you meant when you suggested you weren't the only cheap opportunist in the family?'

He nodded, his eyes narrowed painfully at the thought. 'Your grandfather denied my mother, Andrew and I a decent life. We were penniless. My mother had no head for business, didn't understand how one minute we had money, the next nothing. She couldn't cope; it killed her.'

'And...and you and Andrew...the orphanages?' Her eyes filled with tears. 'Oh, Sam, I'm sorry...so terribly sorry.'

'Can you begin to understand?'

She nodded, jerking tears down her cheeks. She thought of her own luxurious upbringing, never wanting for anything, the best her father could provide for her.

'When your parents are tragically snatched from you, something happens inside you. We were just two kids with nothing. You grow up institutionalised, growing harder with each year that passes, and then, when you get your wits about you, you want to know. Want to know who you are, where you came from. Who were those two people you can barely remember? Andrew said he didn't care, put on a brave face, but I knew it was eating him up as much as me.'

'But how did you find all this out?'

'It took me years. My parents were only children, their parents dead. All I had was a bundle of birth certificates which the orphanages held for us. I traced the family back, went to Canada and discovered my father had once been a wealthy man. I couldn't understand how he had lost that wealth. I wanted to know, had to find out. I came back to England and started delving once again, struck lucky with a bank manager in the town we came from. It was before his time but he came up with some records that intrigued me. Vast payments made out to George Trent.'

'But that wasn't enough. You couldn't have known what those payments were for.'

'I didn't. But my curiosity spurred me on. Solicitors, more bank managers, shopkeepers even. In desperation I sought out old neighbours.' He smiled at Fenella. 'I'll say one thing for northerners, they stick together and keep a close eye on each other. I found an old soul who remembered our family and the young nanny who looked after Andy and me when we were kids. I tracked her down in Manchester.'

'She remembered you?'

'Not only remembered us but had kept all my parents' papers. She had actually tried to trace us but drawn a blank because we had been moved around from home to home.'

'Those papers, were they to do with my grandfather?'

Sam nodded. 'Everything I needed to convince Joseph Trent that I had a stake in Trent Industries but nothing that would stand up in court. Hearsay, your father said when I approached him with them.'

'Seven years ago? When...when you came to the house for the first time? When...when he threw you out?'

'No, a year before. In Northumbria. I marched into his office, all naïve twenty-five years of me. Demanded my rights. He laughed in my face. Said to come back if and when I had more than a handful of dusty old letters to convince him with.'

'And a year later, you did?'

'A year later I had the same as I have now, a handful of dusty old papers. But in that year I had worked and studied the steel industry; it wasn't long enough, not by a long way, but like my father before me I had ideas and a burning flair. I put those ideas to your father, thinking that if he took them on...took me on...' He rubbed his forehead. 'I must have been out of my mind. I thought that if he took me on and I gained his respect he might be encouraged to delve into Trent Industries' archives, maybe find that the Ballantines were entitled to a slice of his shares. He wouldn't hear of my ideas, said Trent Industries didn't need them. In desperation I asked for money, a loan to get me started in my own business—I thought it the least he could do for me.' Sam laughed grimly. 'It was the last straw for him; he threw me out with a flea in my ear.'

'But, Sam,' Fenella husked, 'you came to my father's wedding, you were invited. Joan said you and he were the best of friends. He offered you the use of his home for as long as you wished!'

'He wrote to me, a few months after he turned me away. Said that he'd treated me harshly, admired my spirit and to keep in touch. I did just that. We kept up a correspondence for all those years, became good friends. He came out to Saudi to see what I was up to, seemed impressed.'

'Then you came back, but why? Had he found some proof that you were entitled to a part of Trent Industries?'

Sam frowned. 'I don't know; your father plays his cards close to his chest but he wrote and offered me a partnership. It made me think that he knew more than he was letting on. But the partnership wasn't enough, Fenella. The day your father denied me my rights I was determined to fight back. Somehow I would get back what rightfully belonged to me and Andrew. It wasn't a personal vendetta against your father—he'd done no wrong—but his father before him had ruined our lives. I couldn't forgive or forget.'

'And you still can't?' Fenella frowned at him. 'You still want to destroy him?'

'No, darling, not that, not now. I love you and respect your father too much to hurt either of you.'

'But you are hurting us,' she insisted. 'You told me yourself you want everything!'

'It's the only way, Fenella.' He raked a hand through his hair. 'I had to do what I had to do. I've been buying up small industries, building my own company to an unstoppable force, put myself in a position to take over Trent Industries, lock, stock and barrel.'

'That's ridiculous!' Fenella retorted. 'No one is bigger than Trent's——'

'I am,' Sam told her forcibly. 'I've got your father's back against the wall and he has no choice.'

'That's cruel!'

'Sometimes you have to be cruel to be kind, and there is no room for sentimentality in business.'

Fenella stood up shakily, her nerves taut and fired with anger. 'I . . . I don't know why I came. You're evil . . . wicked!' She snatched up her car keys from the packing case. 'I . . . thought I loved you . . . but I must be crazy . . .'

'Fenella!' Sam got to his feet, reached for her.

'Don't touch me! I never want to see you again!'

He grasped her wrist so tightly that she winced with pain.

'I haven't finished yet.' He swung her to face him and she tensed at the anger steeling his grey eyes to nearly black. 'I admit at first I was motivated by revenge but things changed when I saw the state the company was in, the way it was heading. I had to do it, Fenella, because if I didn't someone else would have done. The Germans, the Japanese . . .'

'Don't be so damned stupid——'

'It's the truth! Another year and Trent Industries would be finished for good without me. Your father was heading for the biggest crash in——'

'The company is as solid as a rock! I've read the annual reports——'

'Read between the lines, have you?'

Fenella's eyes blinked uncertainly. 'My . . . my father lets me go through those papers, he . . . he wouldn't let me do that if there was any fear of the company's crashing.'

'Exactly. He's been blind to it himself, that's why. His profits are paltry to what the rest of Europe are doing. He's outdated, out-moded. He stubbornly refuses to acknowledge new technology. Says the old ways are the best. You must know how wrong that sort of thinking is, Fenella. You run your own company, don't you? You know what you have to do to keep ahead of the next agency?'

Fenella's shoulders sagged helplessly. She lowered her lashes, knowing all he said was true. She knew how stubborn her father could be too. His very refusal to have her—or any other woman come to that—anywhere near the board of directors showed how unprogressive he was.

Sam pulled her into his arms, held her tightly against him. 'Darling, I'm sorry, sorry for all the grief I've caused you.'

'Oh, Sam,' she moaned, still confused and unhappy. She loved this man, had hated him for doing what he was doing to the other man in her life, her father. She understood her father's fears and bitter anger, understood Sam's motivation and why he had done what he thought necessary, and by the sounds of it he was right. But how could they all live with it? She felt as if her heart was being pulled both ways, her loyalties stretched to breaking point. Desperately she clung on to Sam. 'What's to become of us?'

'We're going to be married, of course,' he murmured into her hair. 'We'll give your father all the grandsons and daughters he could ever wish for.' He lowered his mouth to hers and kissed her softly, lovingly.

Fenella clung to him, desperately, returned his kisses with all the hopelessness she felt. Breaking away she sobbed, 'He'll never allow it, Sam. We'll have to elope, run away together... Oh, that would be hopeless... he'll kill you...'

Sam laughed, rained soft kisses on her fiery cheeks, her eyelids, her nose. 'We're not running anywhere, darling. Your father is obstinate, but not a fool.'

'But he has his pride.'

'And I've left him with it, Fenella. Do you think I would rob him of everything?' Her eyes widened hopefully. 'I've spent three long days with him up north. I hired a team of financial advisers to convince him that my plans for the future are solid and without prejudice. At last I got through to him. Trent-Ballantine Industries was born, your father the chairman of our new venture.'

'Oh, Sam, Sam!' she cried, tears of happiness blinding his grin from her eyes. 'But... but us——'

'I left that to the feminine wiles of his wife. I've done enough to disrupt his life for the time being. Telling him I'm determined to marry his daughter whatever he says is tantamount to heaping coals of fire on his head. He needs soothing now but not by me. Adrianna knows how much I love you; she'll convince him I'm right for you.'

'And she knows how much I love you too. She's phoned me every day to make sure I was all right. The whole household has been distraught with worry about us. Oh, Sam, I . . . I need to talk with my father. I need to know how he feels.'

'I know, darling, I know, but not yet. He won't be home for hours yet.'

'He's coming home today?' She laughed. 'You know more about his movements than I do.'

'So long as he doesn't know about mine for the next few hours,' he told her mysteriously, a gleam of mischief brightening his soft grey eyes.

A tiny frown puckered her brow. He grinned at her wickedly. 'Don't you want to see how the house is coming along and . . .?'

'And what?' she quizzed softly.

'I do believe the sun is about to set and I know just the place to view it from. An antique four-poster is installed upstairs, just waiting for the lady of the house to give it her full approval.'

'You're wicked, do you know that?' She giggled happily.

'Wickedly in love with you, sweetheart.' He laughed as he swept her from her feet into his arms and carried her towards the stairs.

*   *   *

She'd talked into the small hours with her father. Listened patiently and understood his reasons for withholding so much from her. He hadn't wanted to burden her, it was enough that he was going through the torment of finding that his own father wasn't the honourable man he'd loved and respected all his life. At first, Sam's story had enraged him, he'd refused to believe it, but Sam's persistence had set him thinking there might be some truth in his accusations. He'd started his own investigations, found the truth, yet pride wouldn't allow him the freedom to accept it. Pride had fought Sam all those years, pride had blinded him till Sam had finally penetrated that wall of northern obstinacy.

Fenella understood how hard it must have been for him and how devastated and bitter he must have felt when Sam had manipulated the company away from him—for everyone's good, her father finally, wearily conceded.

But now, this evening of her engagement dinner with her father and Adrianna, she begged him to tell the truth, that he'd had proof for some years now that Sam had a claim on Trent Industries.

'You must tell him about those papers you unearthed, Dad. It isn't fair to hold them back.'

'He'll get them,' her father chuckled, giving Adrianna a wink over Fenella's shoulder, 'tied up in blue ribbon, a wedding-gift from me to him. I'd have handed them over sooner if he hadn't been such a blustering, arrogant young stripling.'

He poured three martinis; the fourth glass stood empty. They were all waiting for Sam in the study, waiting for him to join them for this special occasion.

'It did him the world of good to get out and learn his trade properly,' Joseph went on. 'If I had given him what he wanted all those years ago he wouldn't be the strength he is today. I knew he had potential——'

Adrianna and Fenella laughed knowingly. It was Joseph Trent's way of admitting to a compromise, taking some of the credit for Sam's drive and determination. Her father was still obstinate but he was softening.

Joseph held his glass up in a toast. 'Here's to our partnership. I think Ballantine and I will make a good team.'

'Hey! What about me?' Fenella laughed, her violet eyes bright with good-humoured indignation. 'I'm going to marry the man, you know!'

'Only if you behave yourself, sweetheart.'

They all turned and laughed as Sam stepped into the study. Fenella's heart lurched excitedly at the sight of him, so devastatingly handsome in his black evening suit. With a wide smile he kissed her cheek, kissed Adrianna and shook Joseph Trent's hand warmly.

Joseph poured Sam a drink. Fenella proposed the next toast.

'A selfish one, I'm afraid. To me and my position on the board of directors of Trent-Ballantine.' She raised her glass and gave her father a smile. 'I've agreed to sell my company and in return Sam has agreed to give me a place on the board.'

Her father looked incredulous for a moment, till Sam whispered to him conspiratorially. 'Until such time as the first infant Trent-Ballantine arrives, that is.'

The two men roared with laughter and Fenella gave Adrianna a knowing smile and murmured to her softly. 'We'll see about that!'

'Now let's go into dinner,' Joseph suggested. 'I do believe Joan has surpassed herself on this auspicious occasion. The smells from the kitchen have had my mouth watering all day.'

'I love you, Fenella,' Sam said softly, hanging back as Joseph and Adrianna led the way to the dining-room.

'I love you too, Sam.' She smiled lovingly up at him. Their lips met in a swift promise of their deep love and commitment to come.

'Dear God!' Sam moaned under his breath as Joan proudly started to ladle the soup from a tureen on the table.

'Your favourite, Mr Ballantine. Fenella worked out the menu. A delicious *bouillabaisse* to start with . . .'

Fenella squeezed Sam's hand under the table and leaned towards him, brushed her lips affectionately across his ear. 'Just to let you know there is one Trent in the family you can't manipulate,' she whispered with a giggle. *'Bon appetit!'*

YOU <u>CAN</u> AFFORD THAT HOLIDAY!

Mills & Boon are offering you the chance to qualify for Free Holiday Spending money worth up to 10% of the cost of your next holiday. There are hundreds of holidays to choose from whether you are looking for adventure or long to lie in the sun without a care in the world – book through the Mills & Boon Holiday Club, details in next months Romances.

SPECIAL INTRODUCTORY CRUISE OFFER
SAVE UP TO 25%!

To celebrate the launch of our Holiday Club, all our readers are offered the chance to join a special 13 night cruise to the Mediterranean and Black Sea, departing from London on 28th September 1992.

CTC Lines popular cruise ship the Kareliya will be your floating hotel visiting eight exciting ports of call, including Lisbon, Athens and Istanbul. Special offer prices start from just £692 per person for a four berth cabin and £999 per person for a two berth cabin and includes almost everything – accommodation, meals and entertainment too!

For further information on our reader cruise phone now on 0533 559855 and quote reference TC9553 – HOH.

AND THERE'S MORE!

One of our lucky readers can WIN this luxury cruise for two just by entering our simple competition featured in November and December Romances and collecting tokens from the back covers.

DON'T MISS THIS OPPORTUNITY OF A LIFETIME – READ NOVEMBER AND DECEMBER ROMANCES.

Next month's Romances

Each month, you can choose from a world of variety in romance with Mills & Boon. These are the new titles to look out for next month.

TEMPESTUOUS REUNION Lynne Graham

A CURE FOR LOVE Penny Jordan

UNDERCOVER AFFAIR Lilian Peake

GHOST OF THE PAST Sally Wentworth

ISTANBUL AFFAIR Joanna Mansell

ROARKE'S KINGDOM Sandra Marton

WHEN LOVE RETURNS Vanessa Grant

DANGEROUS INFATUATION Stephanie Howard

LETHAL ATTRACTION Rebecca King

STORMY RELATIONSHIP Margaret Mayo

HONG KONG HONEYMOON Lee Wilkinson

CONTRACT TO LOVE Kate Proctor

WINTER DESTINY Grace Green

AFRICAN ASSIGNMENT Carol Gregor

THE CHALK LINE Kate Walker

STARSIGN

HUNTED HEART Kristy McCallum

Available from Boots, Martins, John Menzies, W.H. Smith and other paperback stockists.

Also available from Mills and Boon Reader Service, P.O. Box 236, Thornton Road, Croydon, Surrey CR9 3RU.